COACHING for Change

practical strategies for transforming performance

kaye thorne

KOGAN PAGE
London and Sterling, VA

First published in Great Britain and the United States in 2004 by Kogan Page Limited

First South Asian Edition 2005

120 Pentonville Road
London N1 9JN
United Kingdom
www.kogan-page.co.uk

Kogan Page India
2/13 Ansari Road
New Delhi 110 002
www.vivagroupindia.com

ISBN 0 7494 4400 2

This edition is for sale in India, Pakistan, Bangladesh, Sri Lanka and Nepal only. Not for export elsewhere.

British Library Cataloguing in Publication Data

A CIP record for this book is available from the British Library.

Library of Congress Cataloging-in-Publication Data

Thorne, Kaye.
Coaching for change : practical strategies for transforming performance / Kaye Thorne.
p. cm.
Includes bibliographical references and index.
ISBN 0-7494-4400-2
1. Organizational change. 2. Executive coaching. 3. Performance. I. Title.
HD58.8.T4924 2004
658.4'063 – dc22

2004015189

Typeset by JS Typesetting Ltd, Wellingborough, Northants
Printed and bound by Replika Press Pvt. Ltd., India

COACHING
for Change

Dedication

This book is dedicated to the memory of a very special man, William (Bill) Legg, and to his wife Bernice who cared so selflessly for him during his final days and their close friends Sidney and Elizabeth Cole. Thank you all for your friendship, support and inspiration.

Contents

Acknowledgements

I would like in these acknowledgements to pay tribute to my family, friends, colleagues, clients and fellow authors to whom I owe a great debt of gratitude for their ongoing care, support and inspiration.

I would also like in particular to thank the following individuals and companies who willingly gave their time and support in taking part in the case studies:

David Tomkinson, John Kenney, Vincent O'Neill, Claudia Velazco, Deborah Moran, Ian Banyard, Gunnar Brückner and Maria Drago.

Boots Opticians, Siemens, United Nations, Vodafone UK, and the individual clients involved in the case studies.

All the authors mentioned in the References and Further Reading and Alison Church and David Hudnut for their support with contacts for the case studies. All the staff at the CIPD and IOD Libraries for their help in compiling the bibliography. Philip Mudd, Helen Kogan, Heather Langridge and Emily Steel for all their ongoing support.

Finally, all the very special clients and individual learners who ultimately have been my inspiration.

My grateful thanks to you all.

Introduction

Coaching for Change is about using coaching as a powerful tool to support change. Within this context the coaching focus may be one to one, as in personal or performance coaching, team based or about creating a coaching environment within an organization.

This book is written for anyone who wants to transform performance. You may be any one of the following:

- a member of a learning and development, training or human resources function;
- a line manager with responsibility for on-job coaching;
- an external consultant;
- a lecturer in further or higher education;
- a senior executive who wishes to work on a one-to-one basis or with a team;
- an individual learner who wants to change his or her own performance.

Your job role may be a performance coach, facilitator, developer, internal or external consultant, or learning and development trainer or designer. Whatever your title, your interest will be in developing a coaching environment to support and enable change.

How to use this book

This book builds on the key concepts and ideas about training already discussed in previous companion books: *Everything You Ever Needed to Know about Training* (Thorne and Mackey, 2003), *Personal Coaching* (Thorne, 2001), *Blended Learning* (Thorne, 2003a). It is written to support you in your role as you work to develop a coaching environment and is designed to help move from theory to practice.

Special note

While this book is written to help support the development of coaching, it is not a training programme for coaches. There are many professional qualifications for coaches. There are also important differences between coaching and counselling. There may also be times when you recognize the need for specialist support and you may need to identify your own route to gaining support for you and the individuals within your organization.

1

Creating a process of change

Coaching for change is about creating a process of learning that supports each individual's capacity to grow. Personal growth should equate with organizational growth. The corporate effect of individual transformation of performance should be enhanced organization performance, but this will only occur if the individual identifies with the overall goals of the organization.

The reality of this challenge is enormous; many organizations simply have not been able to achieve this alignment. This is due to a number of reasons:

- the quality of leadership;
- the silo effect of different functions competing or not communicating with each other;
- the distance between the leadership and the employees;
- the layers of management that get in the way;
- the lack of sharing of information about the overall direction;
- the willingness to admit mistakes, learn from the experience and move on;
- distancing of human resources (HR), organization development (OD) or learning and development (L&D) from the business;

- the focus on major IT implementation that is kept separate from the people development;
- not fully exploiting the learning opportunities available through learning technology;
- not sharing the learning from different parts of the business, re-inventing the wheel;
- not focusing first on the individual, then the team and then the organization;
- not listening to feedback from the community, customers, suppliers, managers and employees;
- not taking talent management seriously;
- not being brave;
- not being wise;
- not being creative, innovative or championing those who think differently;
- not accepting the challenges and opportunities presented by change.

We could go on; you can probably add to this list, but this is based on the findings of research that I have carried out over a number of years, while working with organizations or as background to the books that I have written. I am not saying every point on the above list occurs in every organization; however, there are equally very few organizations that will not have several of the above issues on their corporate agenda.

The opportunity exists therefore to help your organization rise to the challenge and really recognize what can be achieved by accepting that to survive it needs to do things differently. On a personal basis individuals can also feel threatened by change: it can make us feel uncomfortable; we put things off; we prefer what is known or tried and tested. In recent years we have seen a growth of interest in innovation and creativity, but we still have a long way to go in harnessing the talents of people who think differently and perhaps do not fit the corporate mould.

This book focuses on how coaching can help in the change process; its application is at every level, from personal to team to organization. In this context coaching is about sharing knowledge, wisdom and experience to help in the development of new behaviours, attitudes and skills. Importantly, coaching has to be introduced or further developed into a climate that is receptive and recognizes how coaching can help with the process of change.

It is also about taking coaching seriously, not just putting it on to a menu of training, but embedding it into the fabric of the organization. Way back in time before training was ever thought of as a discipline, people coached. It was the first way that knowledge was transferred. It may not have been perfect and it may have started more as 'telling', but the more intuitive 'tellers' would also have listened, responded to questions from the curious learner and together they would have discovered how to do things and how to make advances in their primitive industries. Coaching today has the benefit of all those years of experience, but it does need a level of commitment to make it happen.

If you are part of an OD, L&D or training function you may feel slightly removed from the process of transformation. In some organizations, following on the wave created by BPR (business process re-engineering) or perhaps the introduction of a major HR or IT implementation, the people development implication can appear somewhat down the corporate agenda.

However, as more and more organizations are realizing that people operate the systems, focusing on enabling the individuals within an organization to transform their performance is an important role for all OD, L&D or training professionals to play.

Being invited to take part or persuading others to let you join will depend on your ability to become a real business partner. Unfortunately there are still too many instances where the learning profession becomes marginalized. In an operating environment, sending people on courses can be seen as a distraction. Engaging the learner in developing real skills to meet business needs, however, is still relevant and important; creating a coaching culture where wisdom is shared can be a positive contribution to transforming performance.

LEVELS OF INFLUENCE

One of the biggest frustrations for any professional is not being taken seriously. If you feel you are a lone voice but speaking with wisdom it is even more frustrating if you feel that no one is listening to you. As with any other influencing situation you need to have a strategy. The first thing is to identify the reality of your own position. Many entrepreneurs or adventurers start with their own idea or belief; then they seek to find sponsorship, funding or other people to support or back them.

You do not need to start trying to influence the whole organization; focus on the parts that you can influence. Explore the concept of change, read about it, identify case studies of other organizations, talk to colleagues and network with other professionals. Knowledge equals power; seek to influence those around you. Have confidence when talking to colleagues or senior managers based on the knowledge that you have gained. All the great writers and business leaders had to start somewhere; they learnt to be persistent, to keep going when others gave up.

Focus on becoming a person with influence. One of the saddest comments that I hear when coaching individuals is people saying, 'I don't think I am good enough', with the result that they have not fulfilled their potential because they live with a fear of failure, or they do not speak out because they believe that others will not listen to them, give them a job or take them seriously. If you are looking to develop others, to build a coaching culture, it is important that you build your own inner resilience, that you are confident, that you develop self-belief and, most importantly, that *you become the person you always aspired to be.*

There are a number of references within this book to becoming a business partner. You may want to use the following questions as the basis of assessing how effective a business partner you could be:

1. Can you accurately describe the current business success of your organization?
2. Do you know what issues in the business would keep your CEO awake at night?

3. What are the current challenges being faced by your business sector?
4. Who are the key competitors?
5. If you had an opportunity to meet with the CEO and board of your business, what would you share as the challenges and opportunities in people development currently?
6. You have been given the opportunity to take a three-month paid work experience/study leave on the condition that you research into an area that could enhance your business on your return. Where would you like to go?
7. Are you in tune globally with the latest trends in learning technology?
8. Do you blend together different cultural and creative influences in your work with learners?
9. Do you regularly undertake stretching personal development each year?
10. Do you have an extensive network of colleagues and business acquaintances?
11. Looking back over your career, do you have examples of work that you have undertaken that could be described as leading-edge?
12. Do you regularly research new areas of development?

As well as helping you to become a more effective business partner, addressing the learning opportunities on this list can help with your own continuing professional development.

STATE OF READINESS

One of the fundamental steps in any process of change is to identify accurately your starting point. This is dealt with in more detail in the Five Principles below; however, it is worth highlighting at the start of this chapter. Talk to any CEO or the person tasked with managing change, and over and over again will come the same issue, 'How do you really make change happen?' One of the biggest issues is people and their willingness to take action. CEOs will say, 'I have done everything I can to pass the decision making down the line' or 'I thought I had empowered my people, but nothing happens; all the decisions still come back to me.'

For anyone charged with transforming performance it is vital to surround yourself with people capable of proactively making change happen, rather than the 'silent nodders' who you know are on the surface agreeing, but underneath are part of the silent majority of observers who in any organization may not actively sabotage progress, but who kill it by their unwillingness to take responsibility for making it happen.

Think about your own organization: how many people have the following profile?

- Positive;
- enthusiastic;
- offer to help;
- willing to learn;
- will try different ways of doing things;
- show genuine interest in others.

And how many have the following profile?

- Negative;
- give the impression of being bored or tired;
- rarely offer additional help;
- more focused on themselves than others;
- prefer to stick to tried-and-tested ways of doing things;
- often say 'It won't work.'

It is this contrast in styles that causes the issues when trying to transform an organization. Many organizations adopt anthems, hold motivational events and build inspiring quotes into the fabric of their company; however, this will make little difference unless there is real belief and unity of hearts and minds behind the words. This can only be achieved through a carefully orchestrated and planned process of change.

Daniel Goleman in *The New Leaders* (2002) talks about true change occurring

> through a multifaceted process that penetrates the three pivotal levels of the organization: the individuals in the organization, the teams in which they work, and the organization's culture. Based on principles of adult learning and individual change, such processes take people on intellectual and emotional journeys – from facing the reality to implementing the ideal. . . the best development processes create a safe space for learning making it challenging not too risky. The experiences have to be different enough to capture people's imagination but familiar enough to seem relevant.

Louis Patler in *Don't Compete. . . Tilt the Field!* (1999) takes a similar approach when he describes the core values approach of Lloyd Pickett of Rodel Inc. More than a mission statement, the Rodel Way is the articulation of a set of principles that have guided Rodel's transformation. There are five commitments that constitute the heart of the Rodel Way:

1. Listening generously: learning to listen for the contribution in each other's speaking versus listening from our own assessments, opinions and judgements.
2. Speaking straight: to speak honestly in a way that forwards what we are up to. Making clear and direct requests. Being willing to surface ideas or take positions that may result in conflict when it is necessary to step toward reaching our objectives.
3. Being for each other: supporting each other's success. Operating from a point of view that we are all in this together and that any one of us cannot win at the expense of someone else or the enterprise.

4. Honoring commitments: making commitments that forward what we are up to. Being responsible for our commitments, holding others accountable for theirs, and supporting them in fulfilling their commitments.
5. Acknowledgement/appreciation: each member commits to be a source of acknowledgement and appreciation for the team; this includes giving, receiving and requesting.

These commitments fill one side of paper and articulate a goal to which everyone in the company can aspire.

You might like to think about your own organization and whether the Rodel principles apply, or what principles your organization has adopted. You may also want to think about your own motivation to change and, although this is dealt with more in Chapter 3, if you are supporting the transformation of performance it is also helpful to identify your own starting point.

SO HOW DO YOU SUPPORT TRANSFORMING PERFORMANCE?

The answer to this can be highly complex, or surprisingly simple, depending on your approach. I have tried to adopt a simple but thorough model of *Five Principles to transform performance*:

1. Accurately assess the readiness to change.
2. Clearly state the overall strategic direction.
3. Identify the key stages on the journey.
4. Gain commitment to the common goal.
5. Establish a process to learn and grow.

If you are looking to transform performance it is important that you identify some key steps. The principles model above is just one suggested model; you need to identify a model that works for you, your team or your organization. At the end of each of the principles there is a series of questions designed to prompt reflection and, it is hoped, highlight some key areas of development that could make your implementation more effective. Choose the questions that are most relevant to your organization; you may want to compare your answers with other colleagues. If you are acting as a coach, identify the ones that are most appropriate in your work with others. The answers can help you build a development strategy.

Step 1: Accurately assess the readiness to change

If you are developing a process for change you need to identify where you are starting from, and quantify the scale and scope of the required change. This can be assessed at an individual, team or organizational level. It is also important to test reality: how achievable are your goals, again from an organizational, team or personal perspective? It is important to look outside the organization. What is happening to your competitors? What legislation may impact on your business? What are the key trends?

Sometimes change can be seen as overwhelming, and this is one of the main reasons why change initiatives fail. Almost like a giant rabbit frozen in headlights, an organization fails to identify which direction to take. Alternatively, individual managers and their teams run off in a set of different directions, each well meaning but totally uncoordinated. Although the perceived scale of change required may seem to be enormous, it becomes much more achievable when scaled down into specific projects or time-frames.

It is fundamentally important to recognize the real starting point. Often organizations involve external consultancies to identify what needs to change, but the same information can be identified from within the organization by undertaking a realistic and honest assessment of the state of readiness of your organization by talking to your customers, employees and suppliers.

It is also important to recognize what has been achieved, what is working well and what can be built on. Step 5 particularly links to this point and emphasizes the need to learn from your current experience rather than keeping on reinventing or discarding current practices.

Questions that you may want to consider

- Looking back over the past 12 months, what have we really achieved?
- What has worked? Where could we have been more successful?
- What development have we offered our employees? Who have been our star players? Who needs more support? (Apply this at all levels in the organization.)
- What feedback have we had from our customers?
- What do our customers need that we don't currently give them?
- What feedback have we had from our suppliers? What service levels have we got with our key suppliers? Why would they want to continue doing business with us?
- Where are we in our market place? What have people been saying about us? What media coverage have we had?
- What are our competitors doing? What other external factors may have an impact on us?
- What about our community investment? What have we done for the community, locally, nationally?
- How prepared are we to cope with change?

Step 2: Clearly state the overall strategic direction

Importantly you also need to identify your level and span of influence. Organizationally who are your sponsors? Can you achieve real change from your position? Depending on your role within the organization you may feel that you have a greater or lesser role to play in planning the journey; however, there are a number of ways that you can become involved.

Wherever you sit within an organization you will have a role to play in the achievement of the overall goals. Transformation teams need champions at all levels within an organization.

You may not sit on the executive board; however, you may be a head of department, team leader or manager with responsibility for others. Individually everyone has responsibility for themselves; therefore in some way it will be possible to identify an overall strategic direction. If you're responsible for others it is important to ensure that whatever goals or overall direction you are setting it is synergetic and linked to the overall strategy of the organization. It is also important that you involve members of your team in the setting of goals to ensure buy-in.

In any process of change there should always be an overall plan, which once decided should be the blueprint for all actions. Just as an architect designs a house taking account of the need for foundations and a properly constructed internal structure, as well as interesting and innovative design features, so do the architects of change need to recognize the need for strong organization foundations and internal structures before embarking on the more innovative approaches to change.

The vision or goal should be very clearly articulated. It should be written in a very clear statement that you and the members of your team can identify with. A test of its validity is that when asked each and every employee can respond clearly to the statement.

People also need support to help them to embrace change; some will be resilient and able to cope, and others will be less prepared and less comfortable with change. Adhering to some simple principles can make the transition more successful.

Questions that you may want to consider

- Do we always consider the bigger picture?
- How often do we take time to think through projects properly?
- Do we consider the following: the strategic implication, the people implication and the customer?
- Do we use planning techniques? Do we undertake SWOT analyses (Strengths, Weaknesses, Opportunities, Threats)?
- How creative are we? Are we hungry for information? Are we curious?

- Are we always driven by unrealistic deadlines or do we build in contingency time that allows for reflection and consultation?
- Do we tend to keep to the same pattern of working, or do we regularly explore new options?

Step 3: Identify the key stages on the journey

As well as having an overall direction you have to identify the key steps that need to be met to achieve the overall goal. These should be SMART (Specific, Measurable, Achievable, Realistic and Timed) and expressed in a language that everyone can identify with. Highlight the key steps but also try and think about each step in detail: think about what needs to happen, what could go wrong and how to deal with issues that might arise. Although traditional tools like SWOT analysis and SMART objectives have been around for a long time they are a good starting point. Have a project plan, and use all the available current project planning tools and techniques to ensure that you can constantly monitor and track where you are with each project. Hold everyone accountable for progress. These stages should be regularly reviewed so that progress can be measured.

Most organizations have a competency model, but the competencies should also include behaviours and emotional and social competencies such as those defined by Daniel Goleman. He defines five basic emotional and social competencies as follows: self-awareness, self-regulation, motivation, empathy, social skills. As well as a focus on the practical skills and knowledge required to undertake roles, there should also be the encouragement of the development of behaviours designed to support personal and organizational growth. These can be simply expressed and measured, eg 'To enable us to meet our goal/vision we need to be able to do the following. . .'

Remember to be creative, encourage people to share ideas, use different techniques to generate different approaches, make no assumptions about the way something has to be done and think about how it could be done differently.

It is also important to build in regular measurement of achievement. The measures of success should be clearly explained. This should build on the SMART objectives and be time-bound. 'By the end of three months, two weeks, one week we will have achieved the following. . .' Encourage people to goal-set on a daily and weekly basis. Use these measures regularly. Don't just set them and walk away; stay close; make them very visible.

Questions that you may want to consider

- Where are we on the journey, individually, in our teams, within our organization?
- Have we matched the competencies needed to the key stages?
- Do we ask who, what, why, when, where and how when testing possible links, and considering all possible consequences of new product development and project management?
- Do we use idea-generating techniques? Do we take time to identify what really inspires us?
- How open are our minds? How often do we say, 'Why don't we try this?', rather than 'We've tried it before; it won't work'?
- How effective are our processes? What could we do better?

Step 4: Gain commitment from others to the common goal

You need everyone to unite behind a common goal. However, you will also need to identify the people who are going to be most proactive; you do not need to call them champions, but in reality they will be the sponsors of the change. You need them at every level in the business from the very top to the newest recruit. They need quietly (and sometimes loudly!) to promote the changes that are required. They will be the people who can keep both themselves and others going when the change runs into difficulties, or when new solutions have to be developed. They will keep going when others say it cannot be achieved; they will be self-motivated, but able to motivate others to keep going.

Others will be able to offer coaching support; build coaching in as a core competence.

Help teams to respect each other's strengths. As the period of change progresses you will need people with different preferences. Use profiles to identify team and individual strengths, and match the right people to the right tasks. Recognize the importance of behaviours: reinforce the positive behaviours and try to eliminate the negative behaviours. Encourage people to share feelings, and support those who are struggling. Recognize, however, that not everyone may be capable of handling the changes required: offer them support.

Questions that you may want to consider

- Do we have commitment to the change at all levels in the organization?
- Have we clearly communicated the vision and the stages on the journey?
- Have we identified the key behaviours?
- Are we building teams of people with different styles of thinking?
- Do we take time to explore how we can work together?
- Do we play to people's strengths?
- Do we share ideas with others? Do we take advantage of global time-zones to work virtually in teams?
- Have we established a coaching support infrastructure?

Step 5: Establish a process to learn and grow

Once the change is initiated you want to build on and learn from the experience. Transforming performance does not require huge resources, but what it does need is often a change of mindset. People need to be prepared to learn from the experience, to share successes and to learn from the mistakes. All too often people move on to something new before reviewing the experience and sharing the lessons. Success can be celebrated at different stages depending on the size of the challenge. It is all too easy never to celebrate because the goal keeps moving. In reality most change processes take many years; therefore celebrating the small achievements is vital in order to keep individual motivation alive.

Questions that you may want to consider

- How often do we review the decisions that we have made?
- Do we allow time to review our assumptions before passing our conclusions or decisions on to others?
- What do we have that works really well that could be adapted? What could we do more quickly? More efficiently?
- When we are presented with a challenging situation, do we take time to explore the 'what if' and develop a plan for contingencies?
- Do we develop a worst-case scenario and plan how we would deal with any issues that might arise?
- Do we celebrate success, not just at the end, but the smaller achievements along the way?

MAKING IT HAPPEN

Once the Five Principles or a similar model for transformation has been established the projects need to be managed; one very real issue for individuals, teams and organizations is how to make it happen.

Right people doing the right things at the right time. Such a simple statement. Think about your own organization: how often does this happen? In step 3 of the Five Principles, matching individual competencies to the tasks was highlighted. An important part of any transformation programme is about helping people identify and develop the required competencies. At the start of the process it is likely there may be three categories of development of the people in the organization:

1. individual and organizational alignment;
2. alignment but needing development;
3. discord.

Individual and organizational alignment

The right people doing the right job at the right time: working with this group as a coach during a transformation process, it will be important to encourage, reward and recognize this group as champions. Ideally they should also be encouraged to take responsibility for making things happen. Take time to ensure that they are supported in what they are trying to achieve. From an organization or a team perspective they should not be held back because of petty bureaucracy.

Organizationally or in a team, this may cause real tensions if it is perceived that certain groups or individuals are receiving special attention. However if you're looking to really transform performance there has to be real change. Just because processes have worked in the past doesn't mean that they will in the future.

As well as sponsoring this group they may also need real support to stay motivated as they may become frustrated with the speed of change. For those who can see the way ahead they may feel that others are deliberately holding them back. As a coach, be sensitive to the needs of the whole team but also recognize the needs of this group. Acting as a sounding board, encouraging them to air their frustrations and helping them to develop personal action plans to manage the challenges that they are facing are important roles that you can provide as coach. Encourage them too to support others; being seen as a star can be a great personal motivator, but helping people to act as a guide for others can also be important. It is a delicate balance between giving them a free rein and asking them to act as role models to help others develop.

Alignment but needing development

With this group it is important to help them recognize where they need to develop. One of the first tasks is to think about the role and to identify if they need to change roles or whether they need to develop new competencies or behaviours. Using profiling tools and competence mapping can be vitally important to identify where the elements of mismatch are occurring. Although this will take time it is an important part of the transformation process, and important to the individual as well as the organization. If the role specification has been clearly defined then this could be a good starting point; if this is coupled with an accurate assessment of an individual's competence then as a coach you can work with the individual to help him or her identify the growth areas.

For some this will mean that they need to develop new competencies; for others it may mean that they need coaching to identify the new behaviours that they need to develop. The work of Daniel Goleman has been mentioned before but using his model of emotional and social competencies can be a valuable starting point. The people in this development category need to identify where the gaps exist and to assess their willingness and motivation to change. This group will need ongoing support; very little in a programme of transformation can be based on the assumption that once it is set up it will happen. Regular coaching sessions, support from line managers and sponsorship from the champions will all help this group continue to grow.

All progress needs to be reinforced. This category may turn out to be the largest grouping in your workforce; therefore they will need constant reassurance and confirmation about the overall direction and progress. When something isn't working out you need to make sure that this group understands what's happening. Changes in direction need to be carefully communicated so that they continue to believe that the change is worth while. When this group is neglected this is often the reason for a growth of discontent or negativity, or disbelief that change is really happening. Lack of motivation and the feeling of a loss of direction and momentum can easily spread.

They will also need assurance that the journey is worth making; although it may take time they will need support to make the transformation. They will want to know that they are making a valuable contribution to the team or the organization, but they will have the highest motivation when they can see that the transformation is worth while for them.

Discord

This is the biggest challenge to any team organization and coach. As with group two, a thorough assessment needs to be undertaken; unfortunately, some organizations lose good people because of mismanagement, or lack of identification of real talent. So when addressing this group the coach has a very important role to play in helping both the individual and the organization explore the reality of the discord. If we look back at the original statement, 'right people, right role, right time', then we will see with this group that one or more of these is out of step. Therefore the first assessment has to be about the individual and helping individuals to identify where they are in their career, what they achieved before they entered the organization, what they have achieved since entering and what they believe their potential to be.

When organizations downsize, individuals often leave without a real understanding of why they are without a job. There is often an underlying feeling of 'Why me?' As an organization transforms there may be genuine mismatches and in this context there will be occasions when individuals recognize that their personal aspirations and the overall organization direction may not be aligned. There may also be a real difference between the skills and competencies of an individual and the needs and opportunities within an organization.

Unhappily too there may be a behavioural mismatch and this is often the hardest element of all. In some industries there will be managers, senior as well as junior, who were recruited and encouraged to demonstrate particular behaviours that now do not fit with the new direction of the business. In Chapter 4 the way people are managed is given as one of the main reasons why talented people leave organizations. If your organization is losing talented individuals this is another important reason to address individual behaviours.

From a coaching perspective working with people who were unable to see the impact of their behaviour on others can be a real challenge particularly if they are senior players. Organizationally there has to be an assessment of how much time to invest in this area of development. Equally important is the impact on the individual: does the individual have the motivation to change his or her behaviour? What is the personal impact on the individual? One of the most important aspects of working with this group is respect and integrity. Whatever decision is taken either by the individual or by the organization will send out signals to the rest of the workforce. Careful planning, careful support and acting in the best interests of all employees are critical measures of the success of any transformation programme, not just for the internal audience but for the wider community too.

There is a need to see people as individuals able to exercise personal choice. Ask simple questions like 'What are you really good at?', 'Given a free choice what would you really like to do?' and 'If you could develop a new skill what would you like to do?' The overall aim should be to create the right job, for the right person, in the right place.

PREPARING FOR THE JOURNEY

How do you and your team share responsibilities for the transformation process?

Team action plan

1. Commit to meeting once a week at a time that is least disruptive and most productive to review all the projects that are in your plan.
2. This should be a session where people are open and honest about the real progress that has been made.
3. Keep to a sensible time-frame for this session; encourage short updates not debate. If there are issues that need real discussion this should be arranged outside this meeting. Use this session to identify resourcing and time-frame issues.
4. Use project planning tools. Having a detailed project plan with an agreed timeline is a vital part of any transformation process.
5. As part of the process, identify exactly what has been achieved, what has slipped and how the time can be recovered. There will be times when there are real difficulties over an action being carried out on time. Teams and organizations have different ways of coping with

this. One approach is to accept it and almost collude with it happening on a regular basis. Another approach is much tougher and not to accept slippages. As ever there is a middle way: the most harmonious solution is to set a realistic time-frame in the first place.

6. This means mapping out the total journey and a really detailed action plan, effectively working through all the actions before they happen, questioning, challenging the assumptions, exploring the 'what ifs' and building in a contingency plan.
7. Tasks are allocated, regularly reviewed and absolutely no assumptions are made. Communication across all parts of the project is well maintained and the best-fit people are allocated to key roles.
8. In this way if things do go wrong there are mechanisms all along the way to ensure that the impact on the problem is minimized. Without this attention to detail, when things do go wrong the impact is much more serious.

DEALING WITH THE UNEXPECTED

If the project really has been planned in detail the incidents of the unexpected may be less dramatic, and so the impact can be minimized. However even with the best planning things do go wrong and it's important that the right resources are deployed to fix the issue. This should be a carefully selected individual or team whose task is to identify clearly what has gone wrong and to seek help and support as required. Sometimes perceived problems and issues can be an excuse for inactivity, and with stretched resources everyone all running after the same ball can mean that problems occur in other areas simply because the focus has shifted.

Giving regular progress reports, communicating on how the issue is being tackled and identifying the lessons learnt can be reassuring and useful, but a policy of business as usual should be maintained for the customers and the rest of the employees.

In his best-selling, ground-breaking first book *Maverick* (1993), Ricardo Semler suggested the following:

> To survive in modern times, a company must have an organisational structure that accepts change as its basic premise, lets tribal customs thrive and fosters a power that is derived from respect not rules. In other words, the successful companies will be the ones that put quality of life first. Do this and the rest, quality of product, productivity of workers, profits for all – will follow.

In his latest book, *Seven Day Weekend* (2003), Semler continues this theme: 'Employees must be free to question, to analyse, to investigate and a company must be flexible enough to listen. These habits are the key to longevity, growth and profit.'

Bennis and Biedermann in *Organizing Genius* (1997) make some very important points about talented individuals and organizations. In their case studies of seven great groups they identified some critical factors about how talented people work together. In their summary of the lessons learnt from their study they suggest the following about recruiting talented people:

> In Great Groups the right person has the right job. . . Too many companies believe people are interchangeable. Truly gifted people never are. They have unique talents. Successful groups reflect the leader's profound, not necessarily conscious understanding of what brilliant people want. They want stimulus, challenge and colleagues that they can admire. What they don't want are trivial duties and obligations; successful leaders strip the workplace of non-essentials. Great groups are never places where memos are the primary forms of communication.

SUMMARY OF KEY POINTS IN THE PROCESS OF TRANSFORMATION

1. Recognize the reality of what you're trying to do.
2. Be brave but not foolish.
3. Carefully research how others have achieved it. Build on their findings but create your own plan.

4. Always keep your overall route map close by, ready to show others and to reinforce your own beliefs.
5. Don't try to do it alone; identify key members of a support team and keep in close communication.
6. Break the journey up into bite-size chunks and set key deliverables.
7. Review each stage and learn the lessons from what has worked and what hasn't.
8. Don't be afraid to amend the plan in the light of the lessons learnt.
9. Don't let apparent difficulties or failure overwhelm you; have contingency plans.
10. People often give up when they are closest to achieving their goals. Take regular breaks, do something different and return with new energy.
11. Listen to feedback but make sure it is balanced.
12. Recognize that not everyone is able to make the journey. Support people as they make the difficult choices.
13. Use your own support network, personal coach and mentor.
14. Do not over-analyse failure; learn from it and move on.
15. Celebrate success and prepare for the next stage of the journey.

2

Creating a coaching landscape

One of the most effective skills that you can develop in your workforce is the ability to coach. Coaching underpins all the great advances of our time, that unique ability to share knowledge and understanding in such a way that the learner takes ownership and moves on. Think of it as a synchronous baton change in a relay race, or the way rowers gain momentum when all the oars touch the water at the right moment and the boat surges forward. Developing a joy of sharing knowledge and wisdom is one of the most natural behaviours that needs to be incubated and developed. Think of the way that a grandparent sits with a child and shares his or her wisdom. Think of the special teachers that you have known and how they inspired your learning. Then think of a normal workplace with all the tensions and pressures and challenges of delivering bottom-line results within a limited time-frame. Is coaching really achievable within this context? Many organizations believe that it is and in its value in developing potential.

The rationale for this book is based on change and how coaching can support that change. The change can be at many levels, organizational, team or individual. Change in an organizational context may be far reaching and part of a global or national strategic plan for transformation. Change may involve the need for a team to operate differently, to work together more effectively or to coordinate their activities with other teams. Change for the individual may be the need to be more personally effective, to fulfil potential or to change direction.

The corporate world is changing quite dramatically. Businesses are facing challenges on an unprecedented scale and the retention of key employees is a major ongoing challenge. Employees equally are looking for organizations that value their contribution. One major way of helping all individuals fulfil their potential is to develop a coaching environment; this is not something that will be achieved overnight, but if you can engender a sense of sharing wisdom you are more likely to create a real sense of personal development. This is very different from the process of 'managing'. Coaching can play a very important role in enabling transformation.

There are key areas to focus on:

1. Identify organizational readiness for coaching.
2. Identify potential coaches.
3. The role of the coach.
4. Develop the right attitudes and behaviours.
5. Equipping the coaches with the right skills and knowledge.
6. Coaching to support the change process.
7. Learn from the experience; share the wisdom.

IDENTIFY ORGANIZATIONAL READINESS FOR COACHING

As highlighted in Chapter 1 it is important to identify whether your organization is ready for coaching.

Introducing a coaching environment may have a very far-reaching impact; individuals need to think about their very best learning experiences, to remember what inspired them, to think about how they can recreate special learning. Managers need to forget about being in control, and instead help their team members to explore by asking open questions and being provocative, and although individuals should never be taken unsupported outside their comfort zone they can be encouraged to push their boundaries beyond their normal learning experiences. Equally trainers could also perform the role of coach and may need to recognize that in the future classroom training may become much more focused on the individual, and as a result small discussion groups or one-to-one coaching may occur more frequently than classroom sessions.

Traditionally coaching was something that might have been offered only to senior executives or fast-track employees. However as more and more people become aware of the benefits of one-to-one support coaches may be found operating at a number of levels within an organization. Another major advantage is that if people really begin to adopt coaching behaviours the organization becomes much more of a learning environment. People really do start to learn from each other, but it needs attention to survive, and this is one of the major challenges. In any large organization it takes constant attention to maintain any initiative. Too many are introduced to an idea, process and way of working, only to find that it is not sustained.

Coaching if it is to be successful has to fit into the broader context of business development within an organization. Importantly it should not be seen in isolation. It represents one of the most naturally evolving processes of developing your human capital. In today's working society individuals are often absorbed into an existing culture rather than create their own working environment. Therefore any strategy to introduce or extend a coaching culture needs to be considered carefully and positioned within the broader context of not just attracting, retraining and motivating talent, but also addressing the business requirements of ROI and cost savings.

You may find it helpful to gain an overall picture of your current coaching environment by identifying answers to the following questions:

1. How does your organization talk about learning and development?

2. Is HR/OD represented on the board?

3. Who receives coaching?

4. How does your organization develop coaches?

5. Is access to external coaches encouraged?

6. Are line managers encouraged to coach?
7. Is coaching a natural and ongoing process within your organization?

An important part of your consideration could also be based on answers to the following:

- How could coaching enhance the development of learning within this organization?
- What benefits could it bring to our overall business strategy?
- How could it help us attract, retain and motivate talent?
- How can it help us to transform our performance?
- What other tangible benefits could it bring us?
- How far have we adopted a coaching culture?

IDENTIFY POTENTIAL COACHES

A coach guides rather than manages; throughout history there have been instances of guidance being given by 'elders'. What if instead of creating 'managers' we created guides? What if we gave respect to the wisdom of our experienced workers? The very best supervisors and managers are those who share their wisdom and give guidance to new employees. The very worst managers are those who play it by the rules with no flexibility or explanation.

What is interesting is that if you examine the development programmes in many organizations it is very likely that you will see references to coaching. However if you probed further and looked at job descriptions for senior managers or members of the board or looked at the performance measures, how often is coaching included? How much real coaching takes place on a day-to-day basis? How is knowledge transferred within an organization? How much real scope is there to create a coaching environment? How much real opportunity is there to reshape the landscape to become more focused on individual development?

THE ROLE OF THE COACH

Coaching is not a passive activity. Coaches tend not to meet with someone and just talk. The most effective coaching relationships are based on proactivity, on action. There also has to be an element of vision and energy, and a belief in the individual, team or organizational capacity to change. Sir Clive Woodward, the England rugby coach, is a great example of someone who not only had to inspire his players but also had to convince the sponsors and the nation that the team had the capacity to achieve their ultimate goal. What is important is the ability to help people sustain their goals even when they do not achieve them at the first attempt.

A coach may also have to overcome resistance or disbelief from the organizational management or the individuals themselves, who lose confidence or feel that it is impossible to achieve a dream. This is often particularly true in the context of more significant change. One of the interesting facts about change is how often people give up when they are just in sight of the winning post. 'Most people give up just when they're about to achieve success. They quit on the one yard line. They give up at the last minute of the game one-foot from a winning touch' (H Ross Perot, *The Best of Business Quotations*). 'Every search begins with beginner's luck. And every search ends with the victors being severely tested' (Coelho, 1993).

Here the role of the coach will be critical in terms of giving an injection of energy to keep going. Understanding the process of change can help to sustain an individual, team or organization through the different stages. The change process is dealt with in more detail in Chapters 1 and 3.

DEVELOP THE RIGHT ATTITUDES AND BEHAVIOURS

Coaching could be described as enabling, ie supporting another individual to achieve his or her personal goals. Within this context it uses a skill set that is similar to mentoring or counselling. To coach someone successfully it is likely that you will draw on the following: questioning, listening, observing, giving feedback, and that you will work within a coaching model of support and challenge. Although this mode of coaching is often used by senior executives the approach is relevant to anyone.

The coach, or skilled partner, will delight in your learning, helping you to move forward with encouragement and giving you positive feedback. What distinguishes the experience is that it's different, it's memorable and it forms an important part of your development. Find the right time, the right place and the right person to guide your personal understanding and it will enable you to experience learning that is so profound that the memory will stay with you for ever.

ROLE OF THE PERSONAL COACH

The difference between personal coaching and coaching can be made clear in considering that the concept of a personal coach is similar to the concept of a personal sports trainer; the coaching offered very much focuses on the needs of the individual; it is driven by the individual and often looks holistically at that person's needs as opposed to being purely work related. With an increased emphasis on the importance of achieving work/life balance, encouraging individual learners to acknowledge and address the opportunities and challenges in their overall personal development is becoming more important and appropriate.

Often a plan is worked out between the coach and the participant, which sets personal goals and targets and enables the participant to prepare for and take control of challenging situations. It is often very proactive and the relationship is built up over a period of time, which enables the coach to really develop a support and challenge approach.

Being a personal coach is like accompanying someone on a journey; in this way being described as a personal guide could be more accurate. As in any journey it is important to prepare, to have an overall sense of direction and then to build in special stepping stones. In acting as a guide there is the need to recognize that at certain times the individual will want 'guidance', and at other times will be ready to enjoy a process of self-discovery. Coaches have a responsibility to get close to their learners and to help them to know themselves.

By understanding how people learn and building that knowledge in those whom they coach, coaches are actively demonstrating the saying, 'Give a man a rod and teach him to fish.'

EQUIPPING THE COACHES WITH THE RIGHT SKILLS AND KNOWLEDGE

As a personal coach you will find yourself using a number of techniques, many of which are used in other applications, eg counselling, mentoring, facilitating or managing others. What is important is the way in which you use the right techniques for the right people, and also the way in which you build the coaching relationship so that the individual is not aware that you are actually using techniques, and the conversation feels natural.

A personal coach is someone with whom an individual learner can develop an ongoing relationship, which enables the individual to explore his or her personal thoughts in more depth, someone who will help the individual to achieve insights and who will continue to be there for the individual over a period of time.

The key point about coaching is that when it is done well it achieves the following:

- creates rapport;
- is set in the right environment;
- is part of an ongoing relationship;
- focuses on the individual;
- shares mutual respect and the opportunity to learn from each other;
- the application of higher-level skills/competencies;
- actions are agreed and followed up.

The most skilled coaches have enhanced skills of questioning, listening and observing and consequently people relax and are willing to talk to them. All the skills involved in coaching are based on natural behaviours, showing genuine interest, having normal conversations with people. However, subtly underneath there is a process of asking open questions, listening carefully to the responses and enabling the transfer of knowledge or, alternatively, acting as a sounding board, helping someone to take action and make choices, or problem-solve within a safe environment.

The role of the coach, tools and techniques is discussed in more detail in Chapter 5 and in *Personal Coaching: Releasing potential at work* (Thorne, 2001).

COACHING TO SUPPORT THE CHANGE PROCESS

The change may be driven by a number of factors, for example:

- change of CEO/board members;
- feedback or criticism from stakeholders;
- business results;
- acquisition or merger;
- environmental issues;
- restructuring;
- career progression;
- team or personal goals or targets;
- the need to adopt a more corporate social responsibility.

At a strategic level coaching can help to prepare people before and after a significant organizational change. With ongoing individual or team change a mature and thoughtful coach can develop enduring relationships, which can help sustain personal change. Using training with coaching support can increase the impact of the intervention: training can communicate and illustrate; coaching can support the action and implementation; taken together the process can inspire and motivate. As highlighted in Chapter 1 there are a number of key stages in the process of transformation, and coaching has a role to play at each stage. Coaching can also support the individuals involved in the process. So many individuals have received more negative than positive feedback in their careers. Encourage individuals to build their self-esteem and acceptance of praise for achievements through setting SMART goals and then celebrating success.

LEARN FROM THE EXPERIENCE; SHARE THE WISDOM

For many organizations, teams and individuals there may be examples of change not working. One very real issue can be about communication. Logically and organizationally there should be an overall process built around the model of 'developing an employer brand' (see Chapter 4). However in many organizations change isn't sustained. The process is either too slow or it is uncoordinated, resulting in a lack of commitment from the workforce because to them it is just another spin on the wheel. Therefore at an organizational level it is critically important to develop a process of connectivity illustrating how the business is evolving. In this way change can be normalized and it can be shown how each initiative links to the last. Even if part of the process does not work it is better to show honestly how the organization has learnt from its mistakes and moved on rather than ignoring it.

Taking time to communicate the impact of change is very important and shouldn't be underestimated. Developing an effective internal communications plan can make all the difference in developing a successful change strategy and ensuring 'buy-in'.

Sometimes in this context there may be a need to challenge the change or the timing. This should always be done by using a reasoned argument and with a positive approach. Thinking through the pros and cons of change before implementation means that you are more likely to be able to overcome resistance. Coaching can help enormously in achieving the right activity, by the right people, at the right time, in the right place.

3

Motivation to change

INITIATING CHANGE

One of the most important factors in initiating change is helping learners explore their reasons for wanting to change. Equally essential is that learners need to own and want the change. As a coach you can help an individual explore the options but ultimately individuals have to make up their own mind that they actually want that change. Everyone is different and so as a coach you need to be able to help all your different learners progress at the pace and speed that suits them. As part of this process it is important that you understand the process of change.

One of the biggest issues for individuals is time; they simply do not believe that they have the time to achieve what they want. There is also a constant juggling between what they would like to do and what they feel that they have to do, and personal development often drops down the priority order in the list. This is not just an issue for individuals; it is often reflected in the ways that organizations charge individuals with meeting business goals rather than achieving a balance between personal and organizational goals.

One very important part of any change process is the motivation to change. From an individual, team or organizational perspective, if the motivation to change is low, the chances of success are going to be limited. Individuals also have different approaches to change. In relation to the stages of change below, some individuals will be proactive while the approach of others will be more considered.

Some individuals will be enthusiastic about change; others will be more cautious. When faced with options and choices some will be able to create their own solutions while others will need more support. Some people prefer to work on their own, while their colleagues may be naturally more collaborative. When faced with overcoming setbacks some individuals will feel overwhelmed and want to give up, while others will rise to the challenge and look for solutions. For a coach working with individuals or teams it is important to identify the potential different responses so that you can support individuals by helping them to recognize where their preferences lie and how to respond best to the opportunities and challenges presented by the change process.

When trying to make significant changes in work or life it is all too easy to express a desire to change without the underpinning motivation to make it happen. In an ideal scenario the organizational and team goals should complement the personal development goals of an individual. Where there is synergy, individuals feel much more motivated to respond to the challenges and opportunities in their working environment.

THE CHANGE PROCESS

Many people make heartfelt comments about wanting to do things differently yet fall at the first hurdle. By gaining understanding of the key stages in the change process and their own capacity to adapt to changes, individuals can develop a personal change strategy. There are a number of models that describe the process of change. For the purposes of this chapter the model that I have adopted is the one shown in Figure 3.1.

We will examine each stage in turn.

Overall vision

In order to achieve a significant change it is important to be able to rise above the immediate situation and to see the potential benefits of

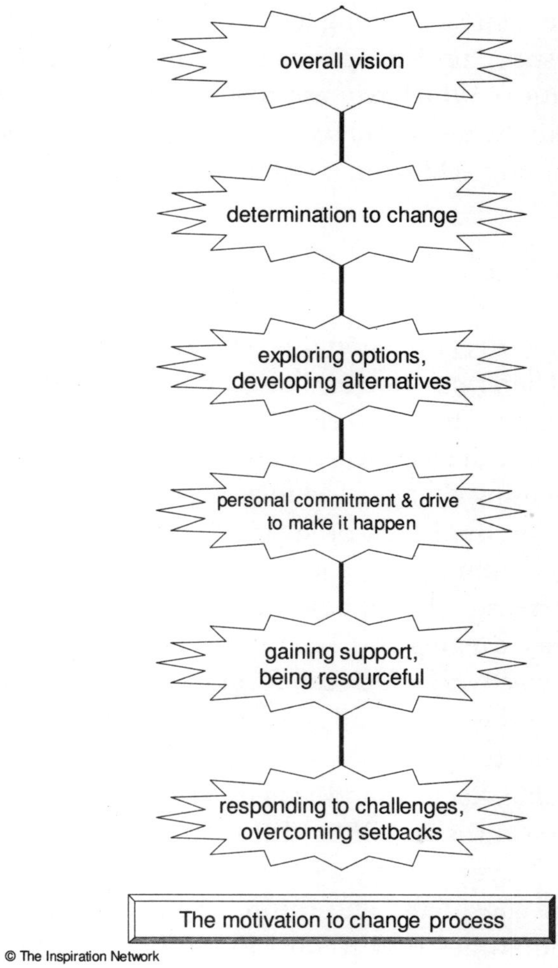

Figure 3.1 The change process

changed circumstances or behaviour. Organizationally it is important to be able to articulate a clear vision of how the future could be and invite your employees to unite behind a common goal. Individually the ability to identify your own work/life goals, or shared goals with your life partner or work team, is an important part of your own personal development. There are a number of different approaches to setting a vision. You may prefer to take a practical approach, for example this statement may apply to you: 'I like to think through all the practical implications before I start something new or different', or alternatively you may prefer to spend time imagining how things could be: 'I like to dream of possibilities.' Whichever approach you use it is important eventually to identify what you're trying to achieve, ideally to write it down and to commit to achieving it within a time-frame.

Determination to change

As well as having an overall vision it is important to have an underpinning desire and determination to change. With this desire there also needs to be an inner resilience to enable you to achieve the change. Organizationally this can be critical because those charged with managing and implementing change need to be able to keep going despite what may be an apparent lack of support and sometimes strong resistance to change from others, some of whom may be in positions of authority. At this stage it is important to be focused, to be able to identify your hopes, dreams and aspirations and express them in a series of focused objectives, which can form the basis of a real plan of action. As well as stating the overall goal, the objectives need to be able to be measured and to follow the principles of SMART (Specific, Measured, Achievable, Realistic and Timed). This applies to life as well as work goals. Again there will be different approaches to being determined to change, particularly related to the speed of change. Some people take a more considered and future approach: 'Although I set myself goals, I sometimes find it hard to motivate myself to keep working towards them', while others have a more direct approach: 'If I want to do something differently I often want to start right away.' It is important to set goals that are realistic and achievable; otherwise you could be setting yourself up for failure. This can apply to individual goals or organizational targets.

Exploring options, developing alternatives

Some people prefer to wait for change to happen to them while others want to be more in charge of their own destiny and sometimes can almost be guilty of instigating change for its own sake. In the exploration stage a coach can act as a very effective sounding board, enabling a learner to explore and chart the options. Some people are also better at harnessing their own creativity and generating options and choices. Often those who are looking for an opportunity to change will spend time thinking and planning a number of courses of action. Useful as you may be as a sounding board it is critically important that the individual takes ownership of the change, particularly if it has far-reaching consequences; without this ownership the individual cannot really move forward. For some people, finding solutions to difficult situations presents a real challenge: 'When I have a problem, I often find it difficult to see beyond the immediate situation' or 'When I have a problem or issue I tend to rely on past ways of trying to resolve it.' Others are more creative: 'What someone else might see as an impossible problem, I see as an opportunity' or 'I often have more ideas than I can actually implement.'

Personal commitment and drive to make it happen

Any change requires effort from the individual. Of course it is possible to sit back and let it happen, but those who have the personal commitment and drive to make it happen will often find that the change is more fulfilling because they have a level of control over the pace and pattern of change by being able to negotiate how it happens. 'When I believe in something I become passionate about it' or 'If I really want to do things differently I can make it happen.' In a coaching scenario this stage really helps to identify those who are prepared to take action compared to those who are unable to move their dream from theory to reality. As illustrated below there is a point that needs to be reached before an individual is really ready to take the first step. As a coach you can help them take that first step, but the individual must have the necessary momentum to carry on. Equally at this stage it is important to keep in touch, as some individuals may also lose confidence after they have taken the first step and, like babies learning to walk, may suddenly sit down and be unsure how to get going again. 'I sometimes give up too easily' or 'I often find it hard to give myself permission to do things differently.'

Gaining support, being resourceful

This is another important stage. Handling change on their own can be a lonely and challenging experience for individuals. Building and using a support network can be a much more positive experience. A coach can be a valuable source of support at this stage by helping people network and identifying other resources. It is important to recognize where someone is coming from. Some creative people find it very difficult to relate to others: 'I often need personal space', 'I would rather not be responsible for other people' or 'I prefer not to share my feelings with others', while others are more collaborative in their approach: 'I have a network of professional people that I use to help me achieve my goals', 'I enjoy coaching other people to help them to find solutions' or 'I have a close group of friends to relax with.'

Responding to challenges, overcoming setbacks

Throughout the whole change process there is an important difference between accepting and challenging the process. Challenging does not necessarily mean conflict, but what it can mean is the ability to take a proactive stance through either instigating the actual change or at least taking an active part in the activities and dialogue surrounding the change. 'If I commit to do something I will see it through to the end', 'I am prepared to take risks' or 'I really do see problems as an opportunity to find a solution.' For others, responding to challenges is much harder: 'If someone strongly challenges me I tend to back down' or 'When faced with a problem I often want someone else to solve it for me.' An interesting contrast between the two styles is what happens if something doesn't work out: 'I can sometimes feel overwhelmed by defeat' versus 'If I have tried every solution and it still doesn't work I am not afraid to give up on an idea and look for other opportunities.' For a coach, helping people to take control in difficult situations is an important part of the personal growth process.

BREAKING THE CYCLE

One of the reasons why people do not achieve their goals is that they never really focus on doing anything about it. It is often much easier to do nothing than to set yourself a plan to achieve your goals. If the people you are coaching are finding it hard to get started you may want to ask them to identify answers to the following questions:

1. What is stopping me?
2. What would I do differently?
3. What could I do today to help me take the first step towards achieving my vision?
4. What help will I need?
5. Who do I know that I trust to talk to about what I want to achieve?
6. What will happen to me if I don't get started?
7. If I decide to wait what are my reasons?
8. If I am going to wait when will it be the right time?
9. What have been the best successes in my life?
10. What can I learn from these successes to help me achieve my current vision and goals?

The answers to these 10 questions could help individuals to move forward to achieve their vision. Each question is designed to help them to think more deeply about the reasons why they want to achieve their vision and goals. There may be a very valid reason why now is not the time for them. This does not mean that they have failed or are not going to be successful. By understanding why they are waiting and the potential consequences, you have enabled them to take control of the situation and make a realistic assessment of their current circumstances.

One of the most fundamental questions they should ask themselves before they embark on any set of goals is: do I really want to do it? If it is a goal that has been on their action list for a while, it is even more important for them to ask the question: do I still want to do it? Sometimes realizing that they can walk away from a goal and set a new one can be a huge release.

As they firm up their ideas they may like to test their readiness to achieve their goals by answering the questions in Table 3.1. Use this checklist to assess their readiness.

Table 3.1 *Checklist of individuals' readiness to achieve goals*

	Yes	*No*
Can they describe their goals in one or two sentences?		
Have they really researched the idea?		
When they have spare time does it readily come to the forefront of their mind?		
Have they refined their goals over a period of time?		
Are they happy to talk about it?		
Could they share the achievement of this goal with someone else?		
Have they got all the information they need about this goal?		
Have they got a network of support?		
Could they overcome challenges in the achievement of their goals?		
Do they *really* want to do it?		

If they have answered yes to all 10 questions then this indicates that they are ready to start to pursue the achievement of their goals. If they answered no to some of them this will indicate areas that they still need to work on.

The secret is: Don't Give Up!

In reality the achievement of their goals may require individual learners to overcome difficulties. The action plan below is designed to help you work through the issues with them and to take positive action to keep going.

DON'T GIVE UP! ACTION PLAN

1. Make a real assessment of the problem. What is it? Why has it happened?
2. Explore options. What alternatives do they have?
3. Remember the theory of right time, right place. Is one of the parts missing?
4. Encourage them to think about their original plan. Have they deviated from it? Have their circumstances changed?
5. Encourage them to make a risk assessment of continuing with their plans. Think of the potential impact of stopping.
6. Encourage them to talk to people, take advice and if necessary ask for professional help.
7. Encourage them to be realistic, to identify what is the real issue. Can they solve it? Can they draw up an action plan to deal with the problem?
8. Encourage them to put the plan into action.
9. Encourage them to monitor their action plan closely and review it regularly to check that they are still on course.
10. Encourage them to think positively, even if they are pulling out. Also encourage them to make plans to re-energize themselves.

GETTING STARTED

One of the hardest parts of trying to achieve a goal is actually getting started. It is very easy to drift, putting off making a start. Often people use external triggers like New Year to try and start a resolution to do things differently, which is fine as long as there is a follow-through strategy in place. It is not just about saying that tomorrow will be different; you need a plan to identify how you will make it different. Setting yourself a target date is also important, using SMART (Specific, Measurable, Achievable, Realistic and Timed) objectives. SMART objectives can be used with any ambition, whether work related, aspirational or personal:

- *Specific.* What is it exactly that you want to achieve? Can you write it in one sentence? If you can't, can you summarize the broad parameters? If you have several goals, can you prioritize in order of either time or importance?
- *Measurable.* How will you know that you have achieved it? Can you write some measures of success?
- *Achievable.* This is one of the most important tests of your ambition. If it is not achievable then you are likely to get really demotivated and, if it isn't achievable, why are you setting yourself up for failure? It is also important to recognize that it may need to be achievable over a period of time or through a number of steps. Sometimes you have to set yourself short-term goals to help you achieve the bigger goal.
- *Realistic.* This is perhaps one of the most important steps. This moves a goal from fantasy to reality. It is no good setting yourself a goal that is totally unrealistic; this isn't about not setting yourself challenging goals, but more about adopting a commonsense approach. One of the failings of some motivational texts is encouraging people to achieve the impossible. While for some this may prove to be the very trigger that sets them on their way, for most of us our hopes and dreams need a surer foundation. We want to be reassured that it is the right thing to do. We want someone to assess the risk for us and, even after we have explored all the options, we turn away and say, 'Maybe next year' or 'I'm not quite ready for it yet' or 'My mother/children/partner need me to look after them' or simply 'I'm too tired to start.' By setting realistic objectives you minimize the risk of backing out.

- *Timed*. When are you going to do this thing? This year, next year, in five years' time? Our society has become much more immediate. In business terms organizations have become much more focused on their annual plans, with outline frameworks for three to five years. What they realize is that the speed of change is so great that it is possible to spend far too much time planning for the long term, when you really need the flexibility and ability to move quickly in the short term while at the same time setting the broad parameters for the longer term. This is a useful approach to setting your own longer-term goals. If you respond well to a timeline approach you can set your goals out based on the time-frame over which you hope to achieve your goals.

PUTTING IT INTO PRACTICE

If you follow the SMART principles you can set yourself an achievable list of goals. If you do apply this technique it is sensible to review your goals so that you can identify if you are on target. There is also a tremendous feeling of satisfaction when you can see that you have achieved something. This illustrates the importance of setting SMART objectives. If they are un-SMART they are likely to be more frustrating than motivational. The bigger your ambition, the more focused you need to be. You need to protect yourself by building around you people who will offer ongoing support.

Far too many people are stopped from achieving their ambitions by others' jealousies or insecurities. This is particularly true in partnerships, whether business or personal. This is where it is important to meet with like-minded people, to have a network and a mentor and especially to know yourself. Everyone I have met who has achieved an ambition has hidden depths. It is partly self-belief, but it is also that ability to self-talk, to say to yourself, 'I can do it!'

4

Organizational change

In today's working environment everyone is having to recognize the need to embrace change. Change is everywhere. Having to work globally, virtually and in the face of new competition, leaders and individual workers are having to cope with new challenges daily. Helping people to cope with change and be flexible and resilient is an important part of any organization development and personal development strategy. Equally important is recognizing the need for organizations to embrace change within a context of constant improvement. Organizations and their management teams have responsibilities; they need to strive towards becoming employers of choice and taking a position of responsibility within their community. One way of doing this is to focus on developing an employer brand.

DEVELOPING AN EMPLOYER BRAND

'Branding' as a generic term is often assumed to belong to the marketing function. However increasingly organizations are waking up to the recognition that directly or indirectly most brand promises are delivered by people not products. Pick up any business magazine that talks about 'branding' and it is likely that it will be discussing the broader aspect of organizational, corporate or employer branding. There is also increasing emphasis on becoming an 'employer of choice'.

What is interesting is how this type of branding is defined. Terms like 'corporate branding', 'organizations as brands' and more recently 'employer branding' are different descriptors of basically the same process. What is clearly being recognized is that having strong consumer brands is not enough; organizations need to broaden their focus to consider other aspects such as:

- people;
- products/services;
- processes/systems;
- premises/environment.

'Branding' an organization means focusing on the key components and encouraging consistency across all functions. As with any piece of machinery, one part cannot operate without the other. Cross-functional working breaks down the traditional divisions between marketing, sales, distribution, manufacturing and HR.

The process links new service/product development and the development of employees. It links the distribution chain with the customer. It builds relationships not just agreements with external suppliers. It takes the most senior managers and involves them in the front line of the business. It puts customers in the centre and heart of the organization and builds everything else around them.

The organization doesn't just service its customers; they become its lifeblood. People do not just make promises, but they deliver, not once but over and over again, consistently developing better and better service. The organization differentiates itself in the market place through its people, its products, its processes and its premises.

In order to develop an employer/organization brand it is important to articulate the image and vision of the future and to invite all employees to unite behind it.

This 'branding' process normally has a number of components (see Figure 4.1). In practice this means identifying the following:

- *Our vision (where we want to be)*. This must be a real statement that people can easily remember and identify with, not just words on a wall.

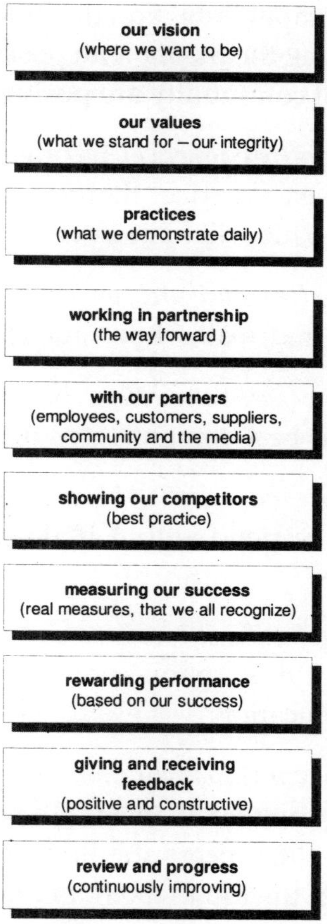

© The Inspiration Network

Figure 4.1 Employer brand model

- *Our values (what we stand for – our integrity).* If these are not daily demonstrated behaviourally by everyone in the organization they are worthless.
- *Standards and practices (what we demonstrate daily).* This is the way we do things, the way our performance is measured; it applies to everyone and ensures consistency.
- *Working in partnership (the way forward).* No person or organization can function for long alone. Working with people, helping others to be successful, building pride and self-esteem and sharing success

are all important components. Equally, building close links with suppliers, encouraging the media with positive news and building links with your local community are positive partnership actions.

- *Showing our competitors (best practice).* Be proud of your achievements, and demonstrate best practice. Be the organization that others benchmark against. This will have internal spin-offs for morale.
- *Measuring our success (real measures, which everyone recognizes).* Never forget where you started; realize how much progress has been made.
- *Rewarding performance (based on success).* Not just money, but personal recognition, which is best demonstrated little and often.
- *Measuring performance (be realistic).* Not 'We promise to do our best' but 'We promise to respond within 14 days, on time, and to meet identified standards.'
- *Giving and receiving feedback (positive and constructive).* From the bottom to the top of the organization (and vice versa), open up channels of communication.
- *Review and progress (continuously improving).* Ask 'What have we learnt?' and 'Where can we innovate?' To prevent a distorted view of the organization, the process should be seamless from the front to the back and from the top to the bottom of the organization.

ORGANIZATIONAL BRAND AUDIT

Here is a way of translating the brand into day-to-day actions by identifying answers to the following:

1. *Organizational objectives*:
   - How are objectives developed and transmitted to employees?
   - How are the objectives measured?
   - What business planning processes are used?

2. *Recruitment*:
   - What messages are conveyed to potential employees?
   - What do our recruitment advertisements say about the organization?
   - How are unsuccessful applicants handled?
3. *Induction*:
   - What process is used to induct employees?
   - How is the company image conveyed? Is it easy to understand and assimilate?
   - How is ongoing induction managed? Is there the opportunity to test understanding of corporate values?
4. *Performance review*:
   - Are job roles clearly defined?
   - Have competencies been defined for the various roles?
   - Are line managers trained to assess?
5. *Employee development*:
   - Is there a clear employee development programme?
   - Does the training function liaise with personnel/marketing?
   - Is the achievement of competency rewarded in pay or benefits?
   - Are managers trained to coach and facilitate so that they can cascade new skills through to their team?
   - Do employees understand that they are responsible for the delivery of the brand promises?
6. *Communications*:
   - Do all communications reinforce the organization brand – both internal and external?
   - Are employees kept informed – clear memos, newsletters and personal letters?

- What messages are being conveyed to our customers and stakeholders?

7. *Advertising/PR*:
   - Is the best use being made of marketing budgets?
   - Is there a systematic review of last year's advertising?
   - Are the results measured?
   - Do our employees deliver the promises that we make to our customers?
8. *Marketing*:
   - Is the marketing strategy regularly reviewed and measured against outcomes?
   - Who is responsible for briefing marketing on the HR/training/personnel issues and vice versa?
9. *Premises*:
   - Does the building reflect the brand?
   - How are visitors greeted and received?
   - When customers/suppliers arrive are the organization's values clearly presented?
10. *Quality monitoring*:
   - What systems are in place to monitor and evaluate the success of the business?
   - If standards are set, how are they measured?
   - Is responsibility for quality delegated?
   - Does each employee feel ownership for quality measures?

Having identified answers to these questions you should be able to put together an action plan, which you can share and discuss with the rest of your colleagues in your organization. This is also something that could be used as part of a climate audit, and the results could form part of the agenda at a workshop for your senior executives.

When asked to describe the brand of the organization, there should be a common belief based on shared vision, goals, aspirations, behaviour and practice.

Everyone who is touched by your organization brand should share these common perceptions. Importantly this is not just an internal process. In the broader context of employer branding it means the way organizations position themselves externally as well as internally. This will have a particular relevance in the way organizations promote themselves in the recruitment market place or in supplier contracts.

The most fundamental part of the process is built on behaviours, based on self-esteem, confidence and pride in the organization. People must take responsibility for meeting challenges and providing innovative and creative solutions to problems. They will then rise above the mundane and gain tremendous personal and team satisfaction from providing excellent customer service.

These concepts are not fundamentally new. What is different is gaining senior-level commitment and linking all the stages together in a holistic way. By bringing all the initiatives together under an organization's 'brand concept', not only is there more coherence but there's a constant benchmark. All employees should ask the question, 'Does this action, this behaviour, this response really reflect the brand?', and in doing so they create an organizational conscience so powerful that organizational success has to follow.

A strong brand image is as relevant to an organization as it is to a product or service. The people offer behind the product has to be consistent with the brand and the commitment has to be reflected from the top of the organization to the newest recruit.

Importantly if you and your organization really want to be seen as a great organization, you need to create your own template of excellence and rigorously apply it, not just once in a while but every minute of every hour in every day.

The businesses that will succeed in the 21st century will recognize that there is a need to do things differently. Value-based leadership, emotional intelligence (EI) and intuition are no longer seen as being outside of the corporate agenda, but are to be understood as an important part of individual and organizational development.

DO WORLD CLASS ORGANIZATIONS REALLY EXIST?

A few years ago I co-authored a book called *World Class Training* (Thorne and Machray, 2000). In our research for this book one of the enduring facts to emerge was that there is no magic formula to enable you to become world class. If we review any of the 'great' companies we will find that each has had to adapt to changing circumstances. Sometimes this was done proactively; however, more often it was as a reactive response to an increased threat, which the company had first ignored.

This is dramatically illustrated by Jim Utterbuck, author of *Mastering the Dynamics of Invention*, quoted in Tom Peters, *The Circle of Innovation* (1997): 'Time after time the industry leader reacts to the threat of change by polishing yesterday's apple.' This was further endorsed by Robert Heller in his book *In Search of European Excellence* (1998):

> The call for cultural change is resounding among the bastions of big European business. . .
>
> Companies like Daimler-Benz evolved a culture brilliantly suited to circumstances, common to most companies until the 1960s that will never be seen again. Market shares used to vary little over time; competition was domestic and played largely by the rules. You made money by maximizing production runs to get the longest possible service from capital equipment and design expenditure. This meant extending product life spans and production technology to the limit.
>
> Economies of scale, rather than economies of method, was the target of top managements. To obtain those economies, centralized control was essential. Individual businesses and brands existed mostly in name. The corporation itself was the real business, and it created a whole caste of managers who served only management itself.

Heller then lists six key factors that today's organizations have to face, which are summarized as follows:

1. Volatile market shares, including fluctuating segments within markets.

2. Global competition, including new players who break all the rules.

3. Variety in production including short runs, marked differentiation, briefer life cycles.

4. Rapid changes in technology of product and process, generating sudden and decisive shifts in competitive advantage.

5. Changing demands of customers have dominated production and altered the nature of selling; distribution has become a crucial component in the ultimate price to customers.

6. Economies of method and exploitation of powerful 'brands' are the joint keys to superior profitability.

Charles Handy in *Beyond Certainty* (1995) also lists similar changes:

> I sense we now stand at the top of the pass. Spread out below is a vast expanse, with no roads through it. We can, I suppose, each take our individual buggies and drive off alone into the night for good or ill. Worse we can jump with some friends into a tank and forge together through the future, and damnation to the rest. Better it would be, I am now sure to build roads on which we can all travel, but that means giving up some personal gain so that all may benefit more in the end. We won't do that, I fear, in our society, in our cities or organizations, unless we have a better idea of what the journey is all about. The Meaning of Life comes to the top of the agenda again, even if organizations want to call their bit of it a Vision Statement. . . The future for us too is in our own place, if we can learn to see it differently, and are 'strong in will' to change it.

Against this backdrop organizations that want to become world class need to be fleet of foot, able to flex and adapt to changing circumstances. Established routines, corporate hierarchies, traditional human resource management methods are all being challenged. Senior management who have grown up with their organizations still resist change; CEOs and their executives react to adversity by going 'too tight', clinging to past successes rather than recognizing the need to build on the past and to create new ways of building for the future.

One of the key features in today's corporate climate is the opportunity that exists for new and innovative organizations to ascend quickly into a prominence as high as that of any of the traditional 'great' organizations. Jack Welch of General Electric once said, 'Great leaders create a vision, articulate that vision, passionately own that vision and relentlessly drive it to completion.'

In my research for this book I found that the challenges remain very much the same. We still need great leaders, and organizations still struggle to create the climate and culture where change flourishes.

HOW TO BECOME GREAT

Key characteristics:

1. Know where you are going; understand the big picture; develop an over-arching plan.
2. Temper this with compassion – recognize your position in the community and address your corporate social responsibility.
3. Be entrepreneurial – seize opportunities to do business and make money.
4. Have a desire and drive to succeed – be energized, committed.
5. Recognize and respect your employees' strengths, talents and emotional intelligence; look to identify the great leaders.
6. Be positive, optimistic; overcome setbacks.
7. Be imaginative, inventive, curious; what shall we do next?
8. Be able to learn from the past, reinvent, regenerate, draw from what is good and discard what doesn't work.
9. Benchmark, measure and celebrate success.
10. Network and partner with others.

LEADERS WHO COACH

How many great leaders do you know? One very real issue for organizations is identifying leaders who have the capacity to lead, motivate and stimulate the workforce of an organization. Leading an organization is no simple task, not least because of the issue of needing to satisfy the business drivers as well as the people drivers.

Daniel Goleman's book *The New Leaders* emphasizes this point and some of the challenges faced by leaders in today's business environment:

> At 'built to last' companies, which have thrived over decades, the ongoing development of leadership marks a cultural strength as well as the key to continued business success. In a time when more and more companies are finding it difficult to retain the most talented and promising employees, those companies that provide their people nourishing development experiences are more successful in creating loyal employees. In short the coaching style may not scream 'bottom-line results' but, in a surprising indirect way, it delivers them.

What is the impact of leadership style on the retention of talent?

In Goleman's earlier book *Working with Emotional Intelligence* (1999) he quotes a landmark study of top executives who have derailed. The two most common traits of those who failed were:

- Rigidity: They were unable to adapt their style to changes in the organisational culture, or they were unable to take in or respond to feedback about traits they needed to change, or improve. They couldn't listen, or learn.
- Poor relationships: The single most frequently mentioned factor; being too harshly critical, insensitive, or demanding, so that they alienated those they worked with.

He contrasted this with star performers: 'Superior performers intentionally seek out feedback, they *want* to hear how others perceive them, realising that this is valuable information. That may also be part of the reason people who are self-aware are better performers. Presumably their self-awareness helps them in a process of continuous improvement.' Knowing their strengths and weaknesses and approaching their work accordingly was a competence found in virtually all star performers in a study of several hundred 'knowledge workers' carried out by Carnegie-Mellon University. The authors of the study stated, 'Stars know themselves well.'

Goleman further develops this theme in *The New Leaders*, suggesting that the singular talent that set the most successful CEOs apart from others turned out to be a critical mass of emotional intelligence competencies. He suggests that the most successful CEOs spent more time coaching their senior executives, developing them as collaborators and cultivating personal relationships with them. From a business perspective, he suggests that those companies where the CEO exhibited EI strengths were the ones where profits and sustained growth were highest, significantly higher than for companies where the CEOs lacked those strengths. He also cites the following research:

> In a tight labor market, when people have the ability to get an equivalent job easily, those with bad bosses are four times more likely to leave than those who appreciated the leader that they worked for. . . Interviews with 2 million employees at 700 American companies found that what determines how long employees stay – and how productive they are – is the quality of their relationship with their immediate boss. 'People join companies and leave managers' observed Marcus Buckingham of the Gallup Organization who analysed the data.

Traditionally organizations have struggled with innovative and creative people, yet look what James Dyson, Ricardo Semler, Richard Branson and Julian Richer have done for their people, their customers and their businesses. Another question in the *Managing the Mavericks* (Thorne, 2003b) research was: 'If you could change one aspect of organizations that would encourage the nurturing of talent, what would you recommend?' Here is a sample of the responses:

- 'Trust people.'
- 'Senior managers being prepared to step outside their conventional modus operandi and/or being prepared to tolerate and/or support others to do so.'
- 'Leadership needs to drive the harnessing of human talent – most companies don't have leaders that understand how to do this.'
- 'Flexibility – understanding that following the "way we do things here" is a recipe for stagnation.'
- 'Recognition (not necessarily reward) for the value they deliver.'
- 'More honest feedback on a regular basis, to encourage and reinforce positive risk taking.'
- 'Let people work *when and where* they think they can offer the greatest potential. It always amazes me that more companies do not let their staff work from home now and again. So much more can be achieved and when they are away from the office and the confines of "its" thinking they can open their mind to thinking in other ways.'
- 'I can tell from my personal experience, the one thing that the organization must do to nurture talent is to provide challenge to the individual, continuous challenge of the individual that stretches him/her to their wits' end is the best "mantra" to nurture talent in the organization.'
- 'Keep management systems simple – the flow chart should fit on one side of A4 in a minimum 12-point font!'
- 'Reward on the basis of contribution to ideas *and* results rather than on grade/project profile/targets alone.'
- 'Values – which is a form of belief. If you believe your people are creative, then guess what? You act that way. Then guess what? They act that way.'
- 'Not overloading people with routine or administrative work. Giving them time to dream.'

In a talent management survey carried out as part of the research for *Talent Management* (Woodhouse and Thorne, 2003), when respondents were asked what support they wanted from a line manager there was remarkable similarity in their responses.

Open and honest feedback was high on the agenda, and there was an important link between freedom to operate and clear goals and expectations. Building of relationships between individuals and their manager is also important, particularly the nature of that relationship. Words used were 'ability to listen, to coach, to offer support coupled with loyalty, trust and integrity'. Alignment of values was also important. One very evocative statement summed up the thoughts of many: 'Foster an environment in which individuals are valued, talent is exposed, nurtured and allowed to fly.'

What is interesting is the balance between freedom and systems. One of the very real issues in large organizations is tracking people. Very often individuals feel that their talents go unnoticed. Equally there are very real concerns that the middle management layer hides and diffuses the impact of real talent. This frustrates both senior management despairing of the lack of initiative and potential within their organization and those new and embryonic talents that get held back because their views may be different from the accepted norm. This was echoed by one of the respondents who recognized that perhaps he hadn't shouted loudly enough – 'my reluctance to shout about my talents means that nobody notices'. What he was looking for was 'real appreciation of my worth by people who are interested in me'.

Equally the importance of ongoing conversations was highlighted: 'Clarity around understanding expectations of individuals and matching these to organizational requirements and having a "real" conversation about this.'

Leaders who coach naturally have an immense contribution to make, and not just in their day-to-day interaction with others, but the more senior they are the more influence they will have on the climate and culture of the overall organization.

Advice for CEOs

Another question asked as part of the research for *Managing the Mavericks* (Thorne, 2003b) was 'What advice would you have for CEOs in terms of nurturing talent?' The common advice to CEOs was as follows:

> Get close to your people; give commitment; follow through; don't give out mixed messages; allow communication to come up through middle management, but actively seek it; don't allow it to be changed and modified by those who do not want others to hear.
>
> Use your people; they are your greatest asset; they are the lifeblood of your organization; much innovation can be generated within; light the candles; encourage the 'speak-up' culture for good or bad. Encourage honest feedback; develop real action from their views; don't ever just take it and do nothing; be seen to respond. Some CEOs find it easier to stick with what is known, rather than attempt to convince long-serving people of the need to change. Some executives are daunted by the size of the task, and the speed of change; some simply hope that, if they ignore it, by some miracle the market will change and the problem will go away.

Innovative organizations do not waste time polishing yesterday's apple; instead they are searching for the apple of the future. Be proud of your achievements; share the excellence and move ahead again.

WHAT IS THE BEST WAY OF MANAGING TALENT?

Senior management are recognizing that their talent bank will be greatly depleted if they do not help people fulfil their potential.

Fundamentally talent management needs attention to make it happen. It also needs a holistic approach. As with customer service, quality standards and health and safety, you cannot just give the responsibility to one person. There has to be a belief and a commitment from the CEO and the executive right through the line management to the newest recruit.

Individuals joining an organization need to feel that they are valued and that their contribution will make a difference. It is easy to say that this is happening, but far harder to have concrete evidence.

In any discussion about talent management or management of high potential it is important first to emphasize the development of all individuals. No organization should focus all its attention on developing only part of its human capital. What is important, however, is recognizing the needs of different individuals within its community.

Talent management is not about a special few people. Real talent management is about playing to everyone's strengths; it is about championing diversity and encouraging creativity and innovation, but above all it is working to create an environment where the organization buzzes with energy and people have a sparkle of anticipation when they enter their workplace.

Being responsible for creative and innovative ways of managing and growing talent can be exhilarating. Individuals also need nurturing. Like plants they should be free to grow, but they need nourishment and daily watering with positive feedback if they are to thrive.

5
The role of the coach

One of the most significant shifts in learning and development is the growth of the role of the line manager as a sponsor of learning in the workplace. As illustrated in Chapter 7, the new styles of learning encompass many different routes, and to support them effectively the managerial and supervisory structure needs to be different.

Traditionally many large corporations have provided training/learning development support through either internal training functions or external consultancy support. Increasingly, driven in part by the growth of leaner organizational models, organizations have recognized the need to focus learning and development through the line management structure.

As head office or centralized training functions have reduced in size or disappeared this has meant a fundamental change in the role of line managers. They have needed to develop new skills and different behaviours. Where organizations have embraced this opportunity and provided their people with nourishing development experiences, there is the indirect impact on the bottom line noted by Goleman (see Chapter 4). This is further endorsed by the comment by Marcus Buckingham of The Gallup Organization that 'people join companies and leave managers'.

If you are developing a coaching infrastructure or are becoming a coach yourself it is important to recognize what this new coaching entails. From a practical perspective there is potentially a limit on the scope and scale of this coaching. As discussed in Chapter 6, the coaching conversations that are carried out in the workplace are limited by the amount of time, the location and the individuals involved. What is important is trying to create a coaching relationship that is as natural as possible; people should not feel that they are taking part in some kind of role-play. The coaching behaviours should become embedded in the day-to-day activities within the workplace.

If we think about workplace coaching and profile the role, there will be certain behaviours that will identify those individuals who most naturally adapt to the role of a coach. There are the attitudes and behaviours that are demonstrated by the very best leaders and managers, and are built on a genuine interest in others.

However, to develop effectiveness as a coach it is helpful to understand more about how people learn, how people react and adapt to change and what motivates people to want to do things differently. This was covered in Chapter 3. From a personal perspective it is worth identifying and understanding some of the tools and techniques used by coaches.

ATTRIBUTES OF GOOD COACHES

- They are trusted and respected.
- They role-model behaviour and live the values.
- They have relevant experience, which adds value.
- They have good communication skills – they question, build, clarify, summarize.
- They offer encouragement and support.
- They take time to listen.
- They let people figure things out for themselves.
- They work in partnership.
- They have a strong belief that improvement is always possible.
- They focus on an end goal.
- They take joint responsibility for the outcome.

THE ROLE OF COACHES

- They build a positive environment.
- They ask questions to analyse needs.
- They use open questions to probe.
- They focus on the needs of the individual.
- They offer suggestions to build on the views expressed by learners.
- They listen actively.
- They seek ideas and build on them.
- They give feedback.
- They agree action plans for development.
- They monitor performance.
- The give ongoing support.
- They focus on improving performance in the current job.
- They assist in raising performance to the required standards.
- They emphasize the present.

CODE OF PRACTICE

It is important that you should also establish your own personal code of practice, for example:

- Respect confidentiality at all times.
- Respond by coaching not counselling.
- Work to create a supportive and appropriately challenging environment.
- Be prepared to build an enduring relationship with the learner.

- Equally be prepared to end the relationship and/or refer on to someone else if you and the learner feel it is appropriate.
- Focus on a holistic view.
- Have the desire to want to model and challenge development.
- Be curious – stimulate curiosity in your learner.
- Recognize that the individual is in charge of his or her own destiny.

This is only the starting point. Before embarking on a coaching role it is important to think very carefully about what it entails and to identify what you believe is important to include in your own code of practice. As highlighted earlier, coaching behaviours are important for anyone to develop either to self-coach or in a relationship with others. It is also important however to seek support and training for the role. This book only highlights key areas to consider. It cannot replace the learning required to become an effective coach.

SELF-KNOWLEDGE

If you are thinking about becoming a coach you may want to consider the following questions:

- How well do you know yourself?
- Can you accurately describe your strengths and areas of development?
- Do you really understand how you will react in different circumstances?
- Do you listen to advice from other people?
- Have you received feedback that has helped you to gain insight into your personality or the way you react to others?
- Are you someone that others turn to?

- Do you inspire trust?
- Do you help others through the tough times? Giving an impression of quiet confidence can inspire others.
- What could you do to be more consistent in your support?
- How aware are you of your communication style? Would others describe you as an effective communicator?
- How easy do you find it to switch off? How often do you take time to socialize with others informally both in and out of work?
- Do you seek to broaden your perspective by taking time to mix with people with different interests and backgrounds, people who may challenge you?

As part of my research into the role of a coach I have identified some key stages:

- *Create the climate.* This stage relates not just to the initial meeting, but also to subsequent meetings. Often when people are being coached for the first time they may be unsure what to expect. They may have very limited experiences of what it is like to be coached. For the new coach too, particularly if it is in the workplace, the surroundings may not naturally be conducive to creating the right learning environment. However with experience a good coach can create the feeling of intimacy even in the busiest conditions. What is important is the attention to the individual and the application of coaching behaviours. A good coach needs to help the learner create his or her vision, and is able to work in partnership with the individual to build an infrastructure to support coaching. A good coach should also be able to contextualize the learning, ie help the learner to develop the right skill in the right context.
- *Build relationships.* The ability to build relationships is at the core of being a good coach. The need to have enhanced interpersonal skills and to develop emotional intelligence is critical in the development of the role of the coach. As mentioned earlier the ability to develop a natural coaching style while at the same time being able to use

different interventions can be invaluable. Transferring knowledge while understanding how people learn can make the learning experience much more effective. Structuring the learning so that you take account of the needs of the learner and adapting your style to suit the learner are important stages in building a relationship. Being open, responsive and having a genuine interest in the learner can also help to build a relationship. Using the right interventions at the right time is another important skill to develop. In a coaching relationship a coach is often accompanying a learner on a journey. It may be a journey towards developing a particular skill, it may be a journey towards achieving a particular ambition or it may be the completion of a specific action plan. Tuning in to the learner and identifying how the learner may be feeling, knowing when to check on progress or simply to call just to remind him or her of your support is an important part of the role of a coach. There is also another important ingredient in a good coach that really can make the difference between success and failure: it is the ability to inspire. There may be many moments when as a coach you doubt your ability to inspire anyone. However ultimately this is what makes the difference in the coaching relationship. It is the intuitive ability to say the right thing or take the right action that elevates the learner into that ultimate achievement of self-belief.

- *Open to experience.* Although not immediately apparent when thinking about the role of the coach this stage is equally important and often is responsible for some of the breakdowns in coaching relationships. Everyone is different and has different hopes, dreams and aspirations. One of the reasons why ambitions are sometimes capped is because of the views of others. Teachers, parents, partners, managers are often responsible for limiting individuals' belief in their ability to achieve something. As highlighted in the stage above, part of the role of the coach is to be able to inspire the learner and so when an individual learner is testing out embryonic ideas with a coach it is important for the coach not to make assumptions based on his or her own experience but to remain open minded and to listen to the ideas of the learner. This is why it is important for a coach to understand his or her own ability to generate ideas, to be creative and innovative, and why sometimes there may be a need to identify with the learner other colleagues who may be able to offer alternative suggestions, advice or support. There may also be a need to help the learner reset assumptions. If the learner's experience to date has resulted in low self-esteem, a coach can help him or her challenge assumptions and help the learner avoid self-fulfilling prophecies of failure.

- *Solution partner*. A coach needs to be able to rise above the issues, to be able to help a learner to work through opportunities and challenges, to act as a sounding board. Coaches work at many levels within an organization. You may be working with a new employee or you may be working with a senior manager. If it is part of a transformation process you may be working with very senior and experienced managers. To be taken seriously as a business partner it is important that you really work to understand what the business is trying to do. Coaches do not necessarily have to have the same professional skills and knowledge as their learner, but they do need to know how to coach and how to help the learner work towards a solution. It is important to be able to have a mature conversation, to be able to offer meaningful advice, to be able to use problem-solving tools and techniques and to help the learner to generate alternatives or solutions. Another important area is to help the learner to manage risk appropriately. Some learners will be risk averse; others may be risk takers. A good coach will encourage the learner to make an accurate risk assessment. Ultimately however the decisions will need to taken by the individual, who has to own the solution. A coach's role is to help the individual to take steps forward, and to support the individual if he or she falls back.

- *Collaborative*. Ideally a good coach can help the learner to network, suggest other support and contacts, help the learner to make connections and if the coach cannot provide the contacts will know someone who can. It is very easy within one-to-one coaching relationships for the focus to remain on the learner or the coach. However most individuals are part of a much bigger group of people and helping the learner to make the connections with others is an important part of the role of the coach. Traditionally mentors within organizations were often seen as people who could provide high-potential employees with the opportunity to meet contacts as part of their development. However there is a much more natural process of communication within organizations, which can enable people to share ideas, build on the experience of others and work collaboratively on projects. It does need to be stimulated, however; it is all too easy for people not to share information. A good coach can link people either individually or in teams to share information and best practice.

- *Appropriate closure/maintain relationship*. This is an important stage, the ability to know how to complete conversations. As identified above, timing is everything in a coaching relationship. In a coaching conversation it is important to understand the point at which to pause or stop and encourage the learner to go and put his or her thoughts and discoveries into practice. Often when people find a supportive coach who is genuinely interested in them, like thirsty plants they drink up the attention and may be reluctant to stop the session. However the learning will be more effective if it forms part of a cycle of input, practice, feedback. This stage takes on a new importance in an ongoing relationship where the learner is encouraged to move forward with less coaching support. In any coaching relationship there will come a time when the coaching relationship has run its course, when perhaps a new coach should be found, enabling the learner to move on while at the same time maintaining contact. Identifying this point and handling it appropriately are important. There has to be a combination of reassurance, encouragement and inspiration to encourage the learner to move forward.

YOUR COACHING PROFILE

Identifying your preferred coaching style can be an important part of your development as a coach. Here is a sample of statements for you to consider:

- *Create the climate*:
  - I am able to create an environment that is conducive to learning.
  - I am able to focus on the needs of the learner.
  - I am not easily distracted by my surroundings.
  - I believe learning can take place anywhere with the right coaching skills.
- *Build relationships*:
  - I have taken time to identify my interpersonal skills.
  - People have given me positive feedback about the way I interrelate with others.
  - I am a good listener.
  - I am able to ask questions to determine learning needs.
- *Open to experience*:
  - I can rise above the immediate situation and see new opportunities.
  - I am not constrained by past experiences.
  - I can often encourage learners to take explorative steps forward.
  - I can inspire others to look at situations in a new light.
- *Solution partner*:
  - Other people often use me as a sounding board for their ideas.
  - I can often see new ways of approaching a problem.
  - I enjoy working as a partner with the business.
  - I can encourage others to work through issues constructively.
- *Collaborative*:
  - I have a network of professional people that I use to help me achieve my goals.

  - Within my organization I work hard to develop networks and encourage my learners to meet with others.
  - I can see the natural linkages between key projects within the business.

- *Appropriate closure*:
  - When I am working in a coaching relationship I encourage the learners to plan for their future independence.
  - Once I feel that I have offered learners as much as I can, I encourage them to develop new coaching relationships.

(The author is currently developing a Coaching Profile to measure preferences when coaching. If you would like more information about this profile, or a Motivation to Change Profile, please contact kaye@theinspirationnetwork.co.uk.)

6
Coaching conversations

Imagine that you had an issue and you would like to talk it through with someone. How would you like that experience to be? Think about the environment, the person, the outcome.

We are all different and our descriptions of the environment and the person may be very different, depending on our preferences. The outcome however may be very similar. Ultimately if we have an issue most of us would want to resolve it. Coaches working with learner colleagues are often asked to help the learners resolve an issue. The issue may be lack of knowledge, frustration at inactivity, or the need to be able to influence a person or a situation.

BUILDING A COACHING RELATIONSHIP

The first step is identifying your coaching skills and competencies. To be able to create a memorable learning experience you need to identify your own skill set and levels of competence. Think about your own style and the way you build relationships. Thinking about creating the right environment for the learner is an important part of the role of a coach. Take every opportunity to create environments that encourage learning. The more natural you are the better the foundation on which to build the relationship. Always be sensitive to learners' needs and, although the environment may be more informal, never compromise on your professionalism or integrity. All the best learning takes place when a climate of trust between the learner and the coach is created. You need to be reassuring about confidentiality, highly responsive and seek to encourage the learner to take personal ownership, to be open in responses and to have a commitment to make it work.

How well do you listen? Do you really suspend your prejudices and listen to others with your whole mind? Often people are thinking about what they are going to say next or making assumptions about the individual or, worse still, thinking about something completely different. Have you developed the skill of effective questioning? Have you developed the ability to ask open questions, to create a natural conversational style when you are able to ask significant questions followed by a process of careful probing? The most skilled coaches have enhanced skills of questioning, listening and observing, and consequently people relax and are willing to talk to them.

One way of developing the skills of questioning and listening is to practise it as often as possible. All the skills involved in coaching are based on natural behaviours, showing genuine interest and having normal conversations with people.

PLANNING THE JOURNEY

One of the first stages in working with a learner is to help the learner to identify what he or she really wants to achieve. There can be a number of contexts for this; it is important to help the learner work through the key stages. For some learners this may prove to be difficult if they have never had the opportunity to sit and review their hopes and dreams. Within a working environment, objective and goal setting tends to be work related, ie what are you going to do to develop competence in the areas that this organization needs?

It will also be important to help the learner test reality. In today's working environment, more than ever before individuals have to cope with and handle change. This was discussed in more detail in Chapter 3. It is essential that you help your learner to really explore the options and not to make assumptions based on what has happened before. This may include helping the learner to make lateral moves rather than assume progress means promotion.

You may also work with individuals who are very happy doing what they have always done; they do not want to change. You may coach people who are suffering from a lack of confidence or self-esteem because of the feedback they have received from others in the past. Helping them to change their perspective may prove to be more of a challenge, because they may see the daily actions of others reinforcing this view.

Other learners may want to develop new competencies or skills, and you may be either directly coaching them or helping them to find the right kind of support.

Importantly these coaching conversations should not just be seen in isolation. We have a responsibility to the individual learners that we coach, in the same way as a trainer has a responsibility to people coming on a training course to help them prepare for re-entry back into the organization, to help them recognize where their team or organization is on their own change journey and to help them develop ways of ensuring their own personal growth as well as supporting organizational change.

If you are acting as more of a personal coach to an individual you can enable your learner to think about what he or she might want to achieve in both work and life goals. An important first step in this is helping the learner to establish answers to the following:

- Where am I now?
- What would I like to do differently in the future?
- What are my work-related goals?
- What would I like to achieve outside work?

Although on the surface these are comparatively simple questions, underneath each question there is a subset of questions to enable you and the learner to identify the learner's current situation and future aspirations:

- *Where am I now?*
  - What skills, competencies have I achieved?
  - What job role?

  - What about development on the job, off job?
  - Who offers me support currently?
- *What would I like to do differently in the future?*
  - What style and pattern of working?
  - What new responsibilities?
  - What job change?
  - Do I want to transfer to another part of the business?
  - What about location?
  - What skills, competencies, training or new learning do I need?
- *What are my work-related goals?*
  - In three months' time I would like to have. . .
  - In six months' time I would like to have. . .
  - In 12 months' time I would like to have. . .
  - How would I break these goals down into SMART objectives?
  - How could I push myself further?
- *What would I like to achieve outside work?*
  - What are my hopes and aspirations?
  - What is realistic to achieve in the short term?
  - How could I break these down into bite-sized achievable goals?
  - Who will offer me support?
  - How will I measure my success?

One of the realities in objective and goal setting is that it is all too easy to set goals and to break these goals down into SMART objectives and yet still not to achieve anything beyond this first stage in the activity. The reason for this is that many people find it hard to kick-start themselves out of their current situation, so a very real question might be 'What is stopping you?'

There are a number of possible reasons:

- inertia;
- fear of moving outside their own comfort zone;
- low self-esteem;
- workload;
- lack of motivation, self-belief;
- no real desire to do anything different.

This is reflected by the well-known saying, 'If you do what you always did you'll get what you always got.'

Often individuals get caught in patterns of working and behaving that are reinforced by the people and situations around them. Encouraging them to take the important first step is an essential part of the role of being a coach. As in any comparable form of sports or ambition, coaching is about encouraging the individual to move forward by focusing on self-belief and taking the first tentative steps forward. Sometimes it may be the actions of others that are causing the delay; this is a harder issue to deal with, particularly if it is part of an organizational culture. If you are looking to develop talent to support change, having individuals feeling frustrated by bureaucracy or the actions of their managers can result in lack of motivation, inactivity or, in the worst case, talented individuals leaving the organization.

SETTING STRETCH GOALS

One way of helping individuals is to use visualization to encourage them to set personal goals. Encourage them to imagine that they have achieved their goals and to describe what it feels like. Ask them to really explore how it feels and what is different about this new vision from where they are currently. Encourage them to write about this new place and make notes about how it could be. Then ask them to think about the key steps needed to get them from where they are now to where they want to be.

This goal setting should be undertaken in a context of the short, medium and longer term. Again help individuals to succeed by encouraging them to set small targets that are achievable as well as more aspirational and long-term goals. Use techniques such as SMART to help them identify the specifics. You may also need to have some examples to help them build their own set. By asking open questions you can help individuals begin to identify areas that they wish to work on.

Remember, if they are unused to setting goals, seeing different alternatives will take time. Asking an open question such as 'What would you like to do in the future?' of an adult can be as threatening as asking a young person, 'What do you want to do when you leave school?' They simply may not know. It can be more helpful to start with some specifics.

As well as working through goal-setting SMART objectives and helping individual learners shift their paradigms you will also have the opportunity to work with individuals who really want to take responsibility for their own learning. As they grow in confidence you can encourage them to build on SMART by setting goals that are more stretching, but in trying to help individuals develop you need to help them achieve some success. As highlighted in Chapter 3, one other factor is to do with individual motivation. Usually what makes a significant difference in the achievement of goals is that the individual really *wants* to do it.

FROM DREAM TO REALITY

One of the most challenging and yet most valuable roles of a coach is to help learners take control of their own destiny. One of the sad realities is that many people underachieve, often as a result of the feedback that they receive from others. Parents, teachers, friends, partners are often responsible for giving (often unsolicited) advice or feedback that so undermines confidence that individuals give up on a plan or course of action because of doubts fuelled by someone else. What this often does is to reinforce the concerns that individuals may already have.

For a coach the challenge is to help individual learners rise above their own negativity and to resist advice from other people until they have taken the time to really explore how they could move from dream to reality.

One of the first stages in working with learners is to help them to identify what they really want to achieve. There can be a number of contexts for this and it is important to help learners work through the key stages. For some learners this may be difficult if they never have had the opportunity to sit and review their hopes and aspirations. Within a working environment objective and goal setting tends to be work related, ie individuals are often asked to match or develop competencies in areas of organizational need. If you are acting as a personal coach to individual learners you should help them to think about what they want to achieve in both work and life goals.

This is another area where some challenges to assumptions can be made; promotion is not necessarily the way to reward people. For many years there was a belief that career progression meant moving up an organization, taking on more and more responsibility. In recent years both individuals and organizations are beginning to realize that there are alternatives to progressing up an organization. As organizations have grown leaner, downsized, restructured through mergers and acquisitions, traditional career paths have changed. The development of functional specialists, the creation of new business units, the growth of internal consultants and the impact of e-commerce have changed the face of organizational development. Helping learners to identify what level of responsibility they aspire to and looking at alternatives can be a very useful role of a personal coach. Helping them to identify how they can reduce their level of responsibility or develop new levels of specialist skill can be part of this.

RESPONDING TO CHANGE

Opportunities to work as a coach with individuals may mean responding to the impact of downsizing, a merger or acquisition, a new role or responsibility or transfer to a new location, or a new boss. It may also be the desire to achieve a new qualification or to set up on their own in business. These work-related changes can also mean that individuals think more seriously about their lifestyle options and choices. This is particularly true in the case of being made redundant, where people really reassess their options and often make major changes in the way that they live their lives. In helping individuals handle change it is important that you help them to understand the process of change and the key stages.

Initiating change

One of the most important factors in initiating change is helping learners explore their reasons for wanting to change. Equally essential is that learners need to own and want the change. As a coach you can act as a sounding board to help individuals explore their options and wait while they make up their minds that they actually want that change. As discussed in Chapter 3, everyone is different and so as a coach you need to be able to help all your different learners progress at the pace and speed that suits them. As part of this process it is important that you understand the process of change.

As coach one of your rules is to help individual learners really think through the consequences of their actions and to help them set up a clear process for identifying and achieving their objectives. Encouraging them to review carefully at each stage of their progress against their original objectives and helping them to refine them if necessary is one way to ensure that when they achieve their goals they still want them.

One of the very real issues for today's organizations is the transfer of knowledge. In creating a dialogue for change, conversations can be a very powerful tool in shaping the pace and form of change. Think of the great orators of our time and the influence that they may have had on others. Then think of most business leaders that we know. What is their influence on others? When was the last time that you had a meaningful conversation with someone, a conversation that encouraged you, stimulated you, motivated you to go and do something, a conversation where you really listened to someone and asked questions because you were genuinely interested in the replies?

Encouraging dialogue between those who have the knowledge and those who do not is the first step, but enhancing the power and impact of those conversations is perhaps a more critical next step.

One example of this was GE's approach to executive development held at the leadership development centre in Croton-on-Hudson. The course was highly participative. The course members were divided into teams and given action learning assignments. At the end of the course they presented their findings to Jack Welch and the other officers. Jack's participation in 'the pit', which was the name given to the well of one of the lecture theatres, was a unique experience. He typically arrived at the end of the course. His appearance was unscripted, without notes. He expected challenges and he wanted active debate. What Jack was offering was accessibility; he often devoted over four hours to the session. When the session was finished he would stay in the bar talking with the participants from the course. Robert Slater, author of *Jack Welch and the GE Way* (1998), distils Jack's advice as follows: 'act like a leader, not manager, use the brains of every worker, keep it simple, embrace change and fight bureaucracy'.

In Chapter 1 there was reference to the work of Daniel Goleman and Louis Patler, who both emphasize the importance of encouraging individual development in a safe environment and developing respect for the views of individuals.

If more organizations encouraged accessibility then the transfer of knowledge would be more natural. Unfortunately knowledge can still be seen as power and very few organizations create the opportunity for people from different levels within the business to share ideas and concepts. Ask many employees about how they would feel if they were offered a one-to-one interview with their CEO or the board and they would probably feel quite nervous, and yet think about the more entrepreneurial business leaders: how many employees are nervous about meeting Richard Branson, or Julian Richer, or Jamie Oliver? These leaders are demonstrating a new accessibility of approach and a willingness to share knowledge and information.

Think about your organization. What opportunities have been created to share knowledge? How many really meaningful conversations take place? One of the real challenges is how to encourage informal and natural learning to take place. Traditionally, particularly in manufacturing or service industries, much learning took place on the job. An experienced worker would take a trainee and train primarily using the transfer of knowledge. The advantage was that the experienced worker was on hand to monitor the effectiveness of the learning; the disadvantage was that the new trainee could also learn all the bad habits of the experienced worker. To develop more consistency in the training, training courses were developed, over time competencies were identified and the training became more formalized.

However in today's working environment a whole range of approaches are used including training programmes, on-job experience, online learning and coaching.

If you want people to transform performance then it's important to help them both individually and organizationally to recognize what is possible in terms of personal achievement.

SAMPLE COACHING CONVERSATION

In Chapter 1 the concept of individual and organization alignment was discussed. Here is a sample of a model of personal development that can be used by an individual to identify key areas of development or to form part of a coaching conversation.

Hopes, dreams and aspirations

By asking open questions you can help the individual begin to identify areas that he or she wishes to work on.

Questions

- Do you have an overall sense of direction?
- Can you articulate your aspirations?
- Do you actively pursue your dreams, or do you see them as pure fantasy?

- Could you convince someone else that they are worth pursuing?
- How much do you want this dream? Enough to sustain the good times and the bad?
- When would you like to achieve this first dream?
- How could you modify or change your short-term goals if there was a greater chance of achieving your long-term goal?
- Who do you know who could support you?
- What opportunities can this organization present to you to help you fulfil your dreams? What are you prepared to offer in return?

Vision, values and beliefs

As well as encouraging the learner to explore hopes, dreams and aspirations, it is always important to help him or her to establish which of the overall aspirations most closely matches his or her personal vision, values and beliefs. Beneath the goals will be the steps that the learner has to take to achieve those goals and beneath the steps are the skills, knowledge and competencies required to achieve the goals.

Questions

- What is your short-term vision?
- What is important to you?
- How well do you understand your inner values? What do you believe in?
- How do you make judgements?
- How do you feel if your values are compromised?
- Do you believe in 'putting something back' into society?
- Do you feel that the values of the organization are aligned with your values?

Health and personal energy, resilience, drive

Increasingly, maintaining good health is vital in people's working environment. The pace and style of work are changing; individuals need to maintain a healthy lifestyle.

Questions

- What do you do to maintain good health?
- What do you do to stay motivated?
- How resilient are you?
- What are your coping strategies?
- What do you do in a crisis?
- Can you make things happen?
- What one area would you really like to focus on improving?

Achieving life/work balance

What is important in managing these ambitions is to work to achieve a balance. Many organizations are now realizing the importance of helping their employees to achieve a balance between their work and their life outside work. Encouraging your learner to take a holistic view of his or her life is an important step in identifying how the learner can achieve this balance. This may also involve the learner in discussions with partner and family about all of his or her long-term goals. Some of these questions will relate to areas outside work and may not be appropriate to discuss in a working environment, but the learner may want to consider them, particularly if planning for retirement.

Questions

- Which life stage have you reached? What are your future plans?
- What factors may you have to consider in the future?

- Can you make contingency plans to cope with these potential factors?
- Have you achieved balance in your life? If yes, how will you sustain it? If no, what could you do to make it different?
- What financial implications do you have to consider? Will these change over time?

Building relationships

Organizations are beginning to recognize that managing interpersonal relationships is a core competence in their workforce. It is as relevant in the service that they provide to their customers as it is to team and line management development.

Questions

- How would you describe your working relationship with your line manager/team?
- How do you handle difficult people/situations?
- What personal impact and influence do you have in work? Outside of work?
- How well do you listen? How skilled are you at questioning?
- Do you have a network of people in and out of work with whom you regularly meet?

Achieving satisfaction at work, skills, knowledge, competencies, development needs

For many people this is still an important issue. Their personal coaching focus may start in this area with their desire to improve or to develop new competencies.

Questions

- How entrepreneurial are you?
- Do you know your worth?
- Could you convince someone else to employ you?
- Do you under- or overvalue yourself?
- What are you most proud of achieving?
- How relevant and up to date is your knowledge?
- Who do you benchmark yourself against?
- How creative do you think you are?
- Do you know the role that you could play in the change process?

ACTION PLANNING

Working through some of the questions above is only the first step on a development path. To achieve real change an action plan has to be developed with key actions and dates to be achieved. This plan should be revisited at the start of every coaching session. If the coaching is related to skill or knowledge transfer, the learning should be reviewed at the start of each session. True competence is only ever achieved through putting the skills and knowledge into practice, not just once but consistently over a period of time.

The coaching process can be a very valuable start to a lifelong process of consideration, reflection and action:

> Success begins the moment we understand that life is about growing, it is about acquiring the knowledge and skills to live more fully and effectively. Life is meant to be a never-ending education and when this is fully appreciated we are no longer survivors, but adventurers. Life becomes a journey of discovery, an exploration into our potential. Any joy and exuberance we experience in living are the fruits of our willingness to risk, our openness to change, and our ability to create what we want for our lives.
>
> (McNally, 1993)

7

Coaching the new learners

In every new application of knowledge it is important to think about the essence of the message, to distil it through the coaches, implement, monitor and follow up.

What businesses need is both consistency and personalization. As a customer I want a service that I recognize as consistent but that is also personal to me. The level of personalization depends on the service, but essentially it is at the interface of the transaction that it is critical to get it right. Workplace coaches have that opportunity to ensure the consistency of the learning and development experience while at the same time personalizing it to match the learner's style.

Advances in technology mean that the learning can be delivered in a variety of ways and provide a richness in the learning experience. The whole process can be underpinned with some simple questions:

1. What knowledge and skills do the different groups of our employees need to develop?
2. What behaviours and attitudes do we need them to demonstrate?
3. What products and services are we offering our customers?
4. How can we ensure that we have the right people in the right place with the right knowledge?
5. What tools and mechanisms do we have to underpin the knowledge transfer?

The learning can be provided through any of the following:

- Web-enabled or paper-based information;
- audio-visual information;
- presentations, demonstrations, practical sharing of information;
- face-to-face coaching support;
- classroom or team-briefing training sessions;
- assessment or profiling systems to identify preferences and capability;
- regular feedback, to measure progression from an individual, team or organizational perspective.

What is important is that the learning is relevant. The learning should help the learners adopt and practise the behaviours and attitudes to help transform the organization. It should be focused on all levels of the business. If the business wants well-motivated, adaptable individuals it should present a model of organizational change similar to the one highlighted in Chapter 4 and commit to creating the support at all levels to enable change to happen. In this context learning and development can be simply measured. Is this course, learning programme or activity either going to support the business as it transforms its performance or going to enable the individual learner to develop the right skills, knowledge, attitude or behaviour to enable him or her to develop his or her full potential?

In supporting a programme of transforming performance it is even more important that any development is fit for the purpose. What is amazing is that in some organizations the T&D function is sometimes the last to be involved in the process and so continue to run programmes where the delegates arrive having been told a few days earlier that they are being made redundant, or where they question the relevance of the training. If learning and development is to be seen as an important part of transforming performance then the learning and development department has to be seen as a credible business partner. In Chapter 1 this was discussed in more detail, but it is particularly important when looking to establish new ways of learning.

WORKING IN PARTNERSHIP

A partnership has to be two-way and if you are trying to achieve a different working relationship with the business it can seem to be an uphill struggle. Equally, very willing and interested internal teams can sometimes be passed over in favour of using external consultants. Internal teams often need sponsorship to help them build relationships with the business. However with perseverance, professionalism and a genuine interest in the business, partnerships can be built.

One way of achieving this is to focus on developing the knowledge about your business and by helping your internal clients to focus on their needs. A good place to start is by asking the question 'At the end of the training or learning process what would you like people to be able to do that they cannot do now, or what would you like to be different?' By helping people to think about the future you begin to identify the start of their journey. If it is a significant training or development need you may need to undertake your analysis at a number of levels within the organization.

Within this process you may find it helpful to consider the following steps:

- Identify client/corporate goals/desired outcomes.
- What are the specific business objectives linked to this need?
- How will the development meet those needs?
- What training or learning intervention has already taken place?
- What is working well that we can build on?
- What needs to be developed, improved?
- What new skills, competencies are required?
- Who needs to attend?
- What options for delivery are possible? Do not assume it is a formal training course. Outline the different options.
- Who will endorse/sponsor the learning and development?

- How will you evaluate/measure the effectiveness of the training?
- What information is available about the participants – what do you perceive to be their needs?

Once you have gathered this information you will be in a better position to make an assessment of what could be offered and how the different components could be combined into an overall solution.

Another key aspect will be the financial implications of any intervention and at a time of reducing budgets it will be important to prioritize development needs. One of the criticisms often levelled at learning and development functions is their lack of ability to evaluate the effectiveness of any learning and development intervention and to identify the proposed return on investment, often because the nature of the development is seen to be developing 'soft' skills. One of the first actions should be to identify what happens currently, to find out what mechanisms are in place to measure the effectiveness of any solution. In today's learning environment many organizations are questioning their investment in learning and development. At times of cost reduction a learning and development function can look an easy target.

Every part of an organization including learning and development should always be examining their contribution to the bottom line. The effectiveness with which you conduct the analysis of training needs is critical to the eventual success of your training event. If you miss vital clues in establishing what your client or participants need to learn, the outcomes will not maximize your training intervention/impact. However effective your design, delivery or evaluation, if you have not clearly identified the needs you are potentially wasting your, and more unfortunately your client's/participants', time.

DEVELOPING A SOLUTION

The key criteria are based on the following:

1. Identify the core learning need.
2. Establish the level of demand/timescales.

3. Recognize the different learning styles.
4. Look creatively at the potential of using different forms of learning, eg matching the learning need to different delivery methods and identifying the best fit.
5. Work with the current providers, internal and external, to identify the learning objectives and to ensure that the provision meets the current need.
6. Undertake an education process to illustrate the potential of different types of learning.
7. Be prepared to offer follow-up coaching support.
8. Set up a monitoring process to evaluate the effectiveness of the delivery.

Identify the core learning need

Identify the learning opportunity and recognize the need to provide the right solution for your learner. Increasingly organizations are recognizing the importance of tailoring learning to the individual rather than applying a 'one-size-fits-all' approach. We all have preferred ways of learning and, despite all the research and recommendations to take account of how people learn, many organizations from school to work still continue to provide blanket solutions.

As training solutions evolve into learning solutions the hope is that organizations will begin to recognize the importance of making the learning more appropriate for each individual. One approach to this is blended learning, which provides a great opportunity to really tailor the learning to the learner. Of course there will be common themes, common needs, but there is also the opportunity to look creatively at how the learning experience is designed and to use a variety of media to suit differing needs. It will also be important to consider if there is an opportunity to offer the online learning component of blended learning. Not all organizations have the infrastructure to support this type of learning. Find out what works best in your company's culture.

At this stage it is also important to identify how you are going to create the different parts of the solutions. There will be a number of ways in which the learning objectives can be met, and it will be essential that whoever is responsible for commissioning the solution has the necessary ability to look creatively at all the options. This particularly links to how the learning might be tailored, eg if you have a very generic need it may be possible that an off-the-shelf provision could be purchased. This generic provision, however, could be supported by support coaching by a line manager who could prepare the learner prior to his or her undertaking the learning experience and follow it up afterwards. In this way the overall learning experience will feel more personalized.

Establish the level of demand/timescales

In any decision about developing learning solutions there will always be a need to assess the reality of the demand. However, blended learning represents a real opportunity to respond more effectively to individual demand and as such has an application that is as relevant to an individual within a very small business as it is to a team of learners in a large global company. The very nature of the blend builds in flexibility. As with the development of any learning solution it will be important to gain a real understanding of the shape and scale of the demand, not just currently but also in the future. This highlights the importance of making sure that whoever is identifying the learning needs really understands how people learn so that he or she is able to ask the deeper-level questions to understand not just the immediate learning needs but the future needs too. It will also help if he or she can explore with the sponsor the potential of creatively offering different approaches to learning including coaching support.

Recognize the different learning styles

We know through the work of David Kolb and Honey and Mumford (peter@peterhoney.com) that we all have preferred learning styles. As well as different learning styles there are other factors to take into consideration in the way that people prefer to learn. A learning solution needs to take account of these factors. In structuring the learning solution it will be important to take account of the learning styles of others. It also represents a great opportunity to review and revitalize the full learning and development offer. Ask yourself or your team the question, 'How could we really do things differently?'

Look creatively at the potential of using different forms of learning

One of the first steps is identifying what exists. Depending on your size of organization this can be a comparatively simple or a more complex exercise. In large or global organizations it can be difficult to keep up to date with local developments. Learning and development professionals are a creative breed and a programme that may have been developed centrally may often evolve into something quite different as it is rolled out into local regions and districts, or even into different functions.

'Tailoring' to meet the need of customers can also mean that the approach or content may be different from the original. Equally the wisdom gained through implementation may mean that what is offered is different from the original interpretation. All of this normally represents the healthy stages of implementation and development. However if you are trying to develop a strategy to transform an organization it is important to recognize what exists so that it can be integrated and formulated into new solutions.

Work with the current providers, internal and external, to identify the learning objectives and to ensure that the provision meets the current need

In many large organizations this represents the toughest challenge, particularly if the different provisions are located in different parts of the organization either geographically or psychologically. IT implementation and creating an e-environment may not necessarily sit next to learning and development. If you are a strong advocate of classroom training, a facilitator or a one-to-one coach you may not necessarily look for an online learning solution. The power of blended learning is that it can enable more elegant and bespoke solutions by combining one or more methods. Developing a coaching environment may take the learning out of the classroom and invest it in the line management structure. The secret is to really analyse what the key learning needs are and the most appropriate way of meeting them. In the early stages it may need some really basic examples of how it could work.

One of the challenges may be helping others adapt to the new forms of learning. If you feel that you excel in stand-up training you may be less enthusiastic about adopting different ways of developing others. If you are fascinated by the use of design and technology in developing learning solutions you may be less aware of the different ways that learners learn. However in today's learning environment there have been a number of changes including using the line manager as coach, shorter training sessions and the use of online learning and multimedia packages. Going forward it will be important to help everyone involved with learning and development make their maximum contribution.

Undertake an education process to illustrate the potential of different types of learning

As well as highlighting the need to outline the potential of different types of learning, there is also the need to undertake an education process with the rest of the business; this will need to be far reaching as it will include fellow learning and development professionals, line managers and the learners themselves. Some of the potential issues are likely to be linked to the need to do things differently, and people usually need support with handling change, so it will be important to help people recognize the potential as well as helping them to identify the solution that works for them. There are a number of ways that this can be achieved. It can involve online demonstrations, PowerPoint presentations, small lunchtime meetings or workshops exploring the potential of using different types of training medium or coaching.

Be prepared to offer follow-up coaching support

During a period of transformation there needs to be support available to help the learner work through the different aspects of the change. This support does not have to be through the same person; it could be a line manager who starts the process and continues to monitor progress throughout the individual's development. The individual may also have a mentor, or can be encouraged to talk through life goals with a partner or someone close. There may be an online support coach, peer support teams or different tutors linked to both the online and the classroom development. The most important factor is that when learners feel the need for support they have access to the most appropriate person available for them.

Set up a monitoring process to evaluate the effectiveness of the delivery

One of the criticisms levelled at many learning and development initiatives is that they are not effectively monitored and evaluated. This can have significant impact when the organization is trying to measure the ROI. With something as far reaching as transformation it is important to track the development, the lessons learnt and what improvements can be made. Having an internal learning management system can really help in this process, or some method of tracking and measuring progress on the journey.

SAMPLE APPROACH TO COACHING THE NEW LEARNERS

1. *Identify the core learning need.* Line managers need to be trained as coaches. Identify what are the key components of the learning. In this case, there is quite a wide range, some of which is related to the underpinning skills development, eg communication skills (questioning, listening, giving feedback), theory (background reading,

articles, identifying and practising some tools and techniques, eg SMART, GROW) and practice in using the coaching process and receiving feedback.

2. *Establish the level of demand/timescale*. The company is committed to creating a coaching culture; therefore it wants to train all managers with a development programme that will be delivered company-wide over a two-year period.
3. *Recognize the different learning styles*. The managers will all have different learning styles and the programme needs to cater for this.
4. *Look creatively at the potential of using different forms of learning, eg matching the learning need to different delivery methods and identifying the best fit*. At present, a 'train the coach' programme is being rolled out. The programme lasts three days but take-up is limited, as it is difficult to release managers for that length of time. Therefore a blended learning approach could be an ideal solution. Construct a storyboard or flowchart detailing the key steps and the required knowledge at each step. Some of the theory could be delivered online or using a CD ROM, and could be tested with an online assessment. Video streams of coaching scenarios could be developed with observation sheets as offline support. Following the pre-work, the managers could then attend a shortened training programme to practise the skills, and this could be followed up by coaching support in the workplace. Refresher material could also be available online if at any time managers wanted to go back into the knowledge components. As well as technical helpline support there could be e-mail support for queries that they might have. They could also form a support network online.
5. *Work with the current providers, internal and external, to identify the learning objectives and to ensure that the provision meets the current need*. Present the solution to the learner and refine the offering. This should be in two stages. First, the solution should be reviewed with the overall owner of the solution and matched against the original request and objectives. Second, ideally it should be piloted with a representative sample of people. Sometimes if there is a time pressure this stage can be easily omitted in the rush to implement.

However even if this is the case the learning can be identified as the solution is implemented and feedback mechanisms built in. By ignoring this stage the overall solution may be less effective. Organizations and internal functions can sometimes be in too much of a hurry to present the solution in its finished state instead of recognizing the reality of creation. Time for amendments should also be built into the overall timeline.

6. *Undertake an education process and develop a user-friendly demonstration to illustrate the potential of different types of learning*. As above, recognize that there will be at least two audiences, the original sponsor of the training and the line managers themselves, as well as the trainers currently delivering the programme. All will need to be convinced of the value in undertaking a different process.
7. *Be prepared to offer follow-up coaching support*. With a reduced course component it will be important to support the managers pre-course to outline the objectives, and to be available to give support when they start putting their own coaching process into practice. Make it very clear what help is available, and distinguish clearly between technical helpline support and coaching support. Both should be readily available, particularly in the early days of implementation.
8. *Set up a monitoring process to evaluate the effectiveness of the delivery*. One of the criticisms levelled at many learning and development initiatives is that they are not effectively monitored and evaluated. This can have significant impact when the organization is trying to measure the ROI. With something as far reaching as introducing blended learning it is important to track the development, the lessons learnt and what improvements can be made. Having an internal learning management system can really help in this process.

HELPING LEARNERS TO LEARN

Coaching has an important role to play in helping learners to learn. As mentioned previously it is one of the most naturally supportive ways of enabling others to learn. There are so many ways in which you can develop your own skill set to enable you to help others. The very nature of coaching is based on the traditional ways that people have always learnt. There are the underpinning skills of effective communication, observing, questioning, listening and giving feedback, but now there is also a range of other techniques including online learning, which provide a richness and depth of knowledge that was not possible with some traditional methods.

As you grow in knowledge you can help learners to take the steps along their road to fulfilling their potential, and everyone involved in supporting learners should be aspiring to match the learning to the learning style. What a coaching culture provides us with is the opportunity to review very carefully our learning provision.

SO WHAT IS THE ROLE OF THE TRAINER?

For trainers it is important to identify where their provision fits within the learning cycle. Their input fits within the overall concept of knowledge transfer – inspirational trainers can by the nature of their skills and competencies inspire others through their words and behaviours. This transfer of knowledge we know can be enhanced by helping people learn through their senses. Therefore the more trainers involve learners in their learning the more effective it will be. Although we know the power of learning through doing there is also value in learning through presentation. A skilful and effective trainer's role will be closer to the role of the storyteller who can enthral and prompt deep thought and imagination, but however inspiring the trainer is the limit of this presentation should be about 20 minutes.

A trainer designing and orchestrating a perfectly balanced event will need to provide a wide range of learning opportunities. Unfortunately too many learners are still being subjected to large classrooms of training content delivery that only really serves the purpose of recording attendance, ie my body is in the room, but my mind and spirit are elsewhere.

The real role of the trainer is to recognize what the learner really needs to learn through classroom learning and to identify the value-added benefits. As part of this analysis it will also be important to look at each area of content and ask the question: what is the most effective way of delivering this learning? In addition it is necessary also to look at the overall content and to identify whether during the whole event the needs of different learning styles are met.

ROLE OF THE LINE MANAGER

Increasingly line managers are being encouraged to play a role in learning and development. Being developed as coaches could provide very helpful support to line managers. Using a combination of learning could ensure that line managers are able to tailor and focus the learning to meet the needs of the whole team. Developing the macro-enabling skills of facilitation, coaching and giving feedback could provide line managers with a set of core skills that can be used in a variety of situations. As part of this development, if they are also encouraged to practise questioning, listening and observing they will feel better equipped to identify the real development needs of their team. Finding the right solution could be a combination of using internal and external provision, online learning and their own coaching support as the learner puts it into practice.

One of the issues for line managers, in the same way as for anyone else in the business, will be the identification of the relevant sources of learning and development. Accessibility of online learning can particularly be an issue unless the company provides an infrastructure for this in terms of appropriate technological support. This will be an issue with online learning even more than with other forms of learning. Coaching however can provide a very effective way of transferring knowledge. Line managers will need support and development to understand and really develop the skills of coaching. However once developed they are skills that have a wide range of applications.

8

Practical strategies for transforming performance – case studies

In this chapter there are examples of case studies from individuals and organizations that have used coaching to support change. When you are supporting coaching for change it is important to recognize that every individual and organization is unique. While you may find similar situations or circumstances it is really important that you explore the reality of the situation and that you listen carefully to individuals and never make assumptions based on past experiences.

The real joy in coaching is using all your experience to focus on the needs of others, to act as a guide or a facilitator in enabling others to discover their full potential.

I am particularly grateful to the individuals and companies below for their support in taking part in the case studies.

CASE STUDY 1

What was the business issue?

Within the Opticians business of Boots, there was a need to grow sales by differentiating our customer service, in an increasingly competitive market place. One of the barriers to this was a history of a primarily autocratic management style used by most of our managers. We needed to change this from 'tell' to 'coach', to release the potential of the store teams and to empower them to serve our customers better and deliver more sales.

Why did we choose coaching?

- Personal service needs empowered decision making, to be able to give all customers what they need – it can't be done by formula.
- There was lots of latent potential within our professional staff (optometrists, opticians etc), who reacted badly to a 'tell' management style, usually from someone younger, with less knowledge and paid considerably less.
- The business model that was being implemented was that inspiring leadership leads to motivated staff, which leads to satisfied customers, which leads to increased profits – one key element of 'inspiring leadership' was deemed to be a coaching style.
- There was poor staff satisfaction across the organization especially amongst the professionals who constantly had issues with the ethics of their profession clashing with a selling culture.
- There was a history of 'GROW' coaching, although often used inappropriately and manipulatively, so it was building on existing knowledge and skills.

What did we do?

Our programme was based on the philosophy of 'increasing ownership to release potential'. This was also the most effective way we knew to sustain something in a business. We therefore:

- Implemented the coaching programme top-down cascade, and also did it with specific groups of managers to speed up the implementation. This meant the executive directors and senior managers going through it first. A planned cascade, followed with enough flexibility to put specific targeted groups of managers through whilst this was happening, to get the best possible results.
- Identified and trained a large group of internal tutors, who then went on to implement the programme. Our role then became one of review, feedback and ongoing development of this tutor 'community'.
- Used a specific version of coaching (the Inner Game) that defines coaching as getting someone to focus attention to unlock their potential.
- Used upward feedback as part of the roll-out, to give individuals specific feedback from their subordinates, to identify the pressure to change. This was completely confidential to start with, and was then repeated annually and included in their performance review.
- Changed the management structure to support the roll-out.
- Ran our bi-annual stores conferences in a consistent style to the roll-out, ie used a coaching approach rather than theatre-style tell sessions.
- Introduced Operations Excellence as a programme following it, which built on the style change and got ownership for basic retail standards.

What were the challenges?

- Giving it enough time to become embedded as a changed behaviour – 'sticking at it!'

- Protecting people whilst they were changing – removing the threat, making it safe to change, 'nurturing'.
- Keeping stakeholders on-side during the inevitable 'hockey stick' of performance, as people experimented with a new or enhanced skill.
- The reward culture recognized old behaviours and couldn't be changed fast enough.
- Changing the focus of the business from head office to stores, when this meant the people sponsoring the programme lost power/control of things themselves.
- Tutors took some time to come on board and we needed to manage the resistance more quickly and effectively.

What were the benefits?

The 'hard' benefits will always be difficult to quantify as they are influenced by other factors. However, there was a dramatic increase in customer satisfaction results from those stores where the management team had been through coaching. There was a significant improvement when we re-measured staff satisfaction and upward feedback. The other benefits that were achieved were:

- Personal development for the tutors.
- Extra life skills for all involved.
- Implementation of huge subsequent change with minimal HR support – the business became more self-sufficient.
- Meeting effectiveness improved dramatically, becoming focused more quickly and getting clearer action at the end.
- A major restructure, including numerous redundancies, was handled with greater dignity, empathy and all-round listening, resulting in the change programme being held up as an exemplar within the Boots group.

What advice would you give to others?

- Coaching isn't just a skill – it is a belief about how humans operate at their best and therefore works best as a larger culture change programme.
- You need a senior-level sponsor for the work, who is prepared to fight the corner when impatience for quick results happens.
- Coaching isn't a quick fix – it takes time to change behaviours.
- Ensure you get enough investment in time and money agreed before starting the programme.
- It is harder to get results when the required change is a 180-degree shift in management style.
- You need to take a whole systems approach to coaching and look at the other elements that will affect its success, eg management structures, reward mechanisms, career progression etc.
- Don't underestimate how much time and money it will take to maintain the skills for new and existing people.
- Build opportunities to apply the skills into the programme.

Contact details

For more details contact David Tomkinson at the And Partnership (tel: 01636 816629; mobile: 07710 003029; Web site: www.andpartnership.com), or John Kenney, Personal and Organizational Change Consultant/Coach (tel: 01509 881212; mobile: 07798 800486; e-mail: woldsjohn@aol.com).

CASE STUDY 2

What examples do you have of using coaching to support change or transform performance?

I run emotional development training courses for schools and colleges with the aim of helping teachers, tutors and support staff to deal more effectively with emotional situations and challenging behaviour. During the programme I run a short coaching session where I demonstrate how to help people broaden their choices when faced with an emotionally challenging situation. When most people are faced with a potential threat they naturally respond in one of two ways, fight or flee, ie they become aggressive (fight) or they become fearful (flee). In today's workplaces neither of these responses is effective in the long term, or appropriate in a context of professionalism.

An example of this approach was a client from further education who found that when faced with challenging behaviour her natural response was to 'flee'. She readily admitted that she lacked the confidence to assert herself around others.

As a result of the coaching this client discovered at both a psychological and emotional level that she had more options available to her than she previously thought or felt she had. Rather than having to choose between fighting and fleeing situations, which were both physically and mentally uncomfortable and harmful to her in terms of stress levels, she soon learnt that she could develop a range of options in between fight and flee, which we labelled the 'flow' state. The result was that she not only felt empowered in this state, but she also felt calmer and more balanced in herself and was able to think more clearly and creatively when she reviewed past examples of challenging situations. More importantly she was able to feel more positive and encouraged about facing challenging situations in the future.

What were the biggest challenges?

Because my client from a very early age has tended to respond passively to 'threatening' situations, she has formed habits of thinking, feeling and describing her perception of life events in ways that maintain her passive nature. As well as shifting her thinking, the coaching also needs to create an emotional shift too. The skill of the coach to move people through emotional experiences in order that they reconnect with the thoughts and feelings associated with each state is key. The nature of the event meant that I only worked with her on a one-to-one basis during a one-day course; it is now up to her to practise what I taught her and continue developing what she learnt from the experience. This requires self-discipline and self-belief, as is true of all forms of development - academic, physical, etc.

How did you overcome these?

Firstly I helped my client create the desire to want to change by making her aware of the consequences of not changing and outlining the benefits of changing. The coaching process creates a shift at both a psychological level and an emotional level that creates a very powerful and long-lasting learning experience. She has a supportive group of people around her who can encourage and motivate her when her ability to encourage and motivate herself is lacking. She also has a link with me via the Internet, which she has used to update me on her progress and enables me to encourage her from a distance.

What have been the benefits?

She informs me that she has approached situations at work (eg public speaking) in a more assertive and confident way and in so doing is developing her ability and improving with each situation. Outside of work she has also made progress. I received an e-mail from her describing how, while taking part in a charity run with her daughter recently, she found the inspiration and the assertiveness to break away from her group who were gently jogging to the finish line to sprint the last 50 metres despite everyone else's reluctance to 'show themselves up'.

What advice would you give to others?

Emotional coaching as with all forms of coaching requires you (as the coach) to go first. It's no good standing on the opposite side of a ravine shouting 'jump' to your client. Effective coaching requires you to bridge the perceived gap between where the person is and where he or she wants to be. There is a multitude of tools and techniques available for coaches to use in order to help someone through transition. The most powerful, however, is the coach's seemingly natural ability to transfer empowering states of mind and feelings that inspire and encourage others to make that leap by example.

Any other comments?

Today we are fortunate to be able to study, reproduce and further develop another person's 'seemingly natural' ability using studies and modelling techniques from fields such as neuro-linguistic programming (NLP).

Contact details:

Ian Banyard MCIPD
Life Change Coach/Trainer, Epona Associates
e-mail: ian@eponaassociates.co.uk
Web site: www.eponaassociates.co.uk

CASE STUDY 3

What examples do you have of using coaching to support change or transform performance?

September 2003 saw the introduction of a Global Coaching Program for first-line managers. This was part of a major change process launched in 2002, a change process with three main vectors – strategy transformation, establishment of a balanced matrix business model, and people excellence.

People excellence, as a complement and counterpart to business excellence strived for via the other two vectors, consists of four interlinked projects designed to blend leadership and involvement in a balanced form of 'distributed leadership' suited to both the balanced matrix and the network organizations of the future, especially in service companies dependent on people rather than products (see Figure 8.1).

'Leading from the top' involved the executive management team in establishing key strategic principles to guide the company over the next three to four years. This was flanked by 1,000 appreciative inquiry interviews at all levels of the organization. The interview results served as the 'dough', which 300 managers kneaded into our Mission, Vision and Values at the international management meeting in November 2002. The same managers walked the talk during 2003, both in town talks in 25 countries and in cascading workshops to anchor the vision and values in relationships and behaviour.

'Leading from the front' picked up the strategic guiding principles – strong leadership, active responsibility, intense cooperation and top performance – as the focus of a staff survey in early 2003. Six hundred reports were generated. Action learning sessions created the follow-up and implementation, leading to more than 400 actions documented in our knowledge management system.

'Leading from the centre' started in November 2002 with drawing the local unit managers (ie those in the crosshairs of the matrix responsible for P&L) from 40 countries into a development community based on peer coaching and their experiences in running international and/or cross-business-unit deals. This was followed up by launching the Global Coaching Program in September 2003. In many change or transition processes,

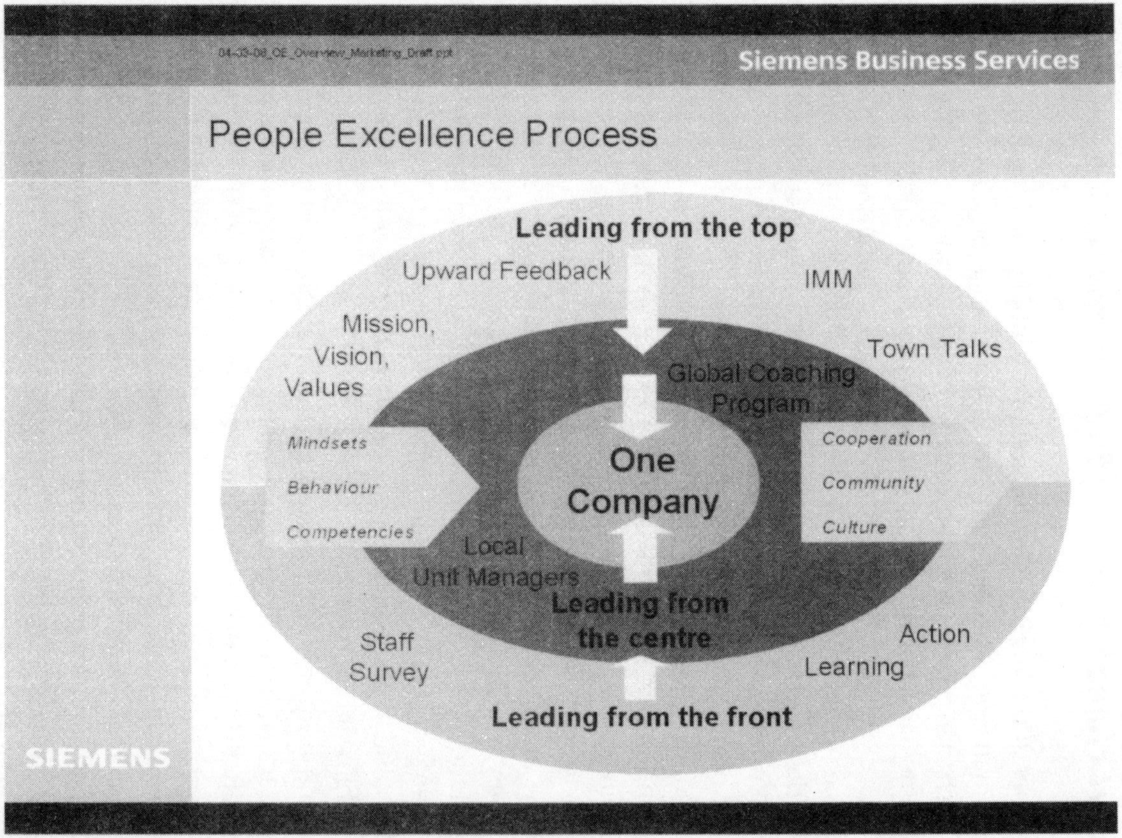

Figure 8.1 People excellence process

middle managers are often either overlooked or deliberately left out, since they are perceived as a source of resistance to change. Our approach was to bind them in by establishing coaching as the key leadership style in the company and developing first-line managers as the highest priority. The programme (seven days, three modules, distributed over six months) focuses on personal effectiveness and performance, combined with implementing the strategy at the customer interface and living the vision and values in staff relationships.

What were the biggest challenges?

The biggest challenge was and is developing a common culture after eight years of constant mergers, reorganizations and acquisitions.

The second challenge was winning investment for a purely people-centred programme when the company had suffered losses year on year from 1996 till 2001.

The third challenge was to make clear to top management how the four projects dovetailed to change the company culture, and to convince them that patience was important, as it would take three to five years to reap the benefits.

The final challenge was shifting the mindset of top management on coaching from a 'remedial' view, through a 'me-too, individual developmental' view to a genuine 'distributed leadership' view aimed at equipping middle managers to coach first their people and then the organization – in other words, to act as the 'transmission belt' of strategic change.

How did you overcome these?

1. By engaging the executive management team in writing individually an 80-page homework book called 'Framework for Renewal', and deriving with them the strategic guiding principles as their common mindset.

2. By involving them in appreciative inquiry interviews – each executive interviewed five people in the organization for two hours and was interviewed by those five for two hours – to discover how to leverage the guiding principles. These two approaches led to a strong commitment to walk the talk.

3. By involving the entire international management (plus more than 2,000 employees via an intranet questionnaire) in establishing our vision and values.
4. By consistency of message, surfacing the areas for improvement related to the four guiding principles via a staff survey, which 14,000 employees took part in, and over 400 documented actions arose relating to leadership, responsibility, cooperation and performance.
5. By successfully forming a networked community of local unit managers to design their own development and show the advantages of peer coaching across a matrix organization.
6. On the basis of the above, by convincing top management that a coaching, dialogue and feedback culture is essential for success in a service and people company.

What have been the benefits?

- Fiscal years 2002 and 2003 showed a profit for the first time in the company's eight-year history.
- 'Distributed leadership' is being established as a mindset throughout the company, and as the most effective and efficient way to leverage the balanced matrix.
- Within this concept, coaching has come to be regarded as the core leadership style for the company, leading to piloting the Global Coaching Program for line managers from September 2003 till March 2004.
- Via 360-degree feedback and other metrics, the 36 participants from 11 countries have shown measurable results in ROI with regard to productivity, quality and the bottom line.

What advice would you give to others?

As technology and price become more similar, as the options for customers and consumers increase and as cost cutting is finite if you do not want to strangle a company entirely, the importance of ROHI (return on human investment) becomes key.

Investment in people in terms of meaning, in terms of distributed leadership, in terms of values will make the difference between success and failure. Balancing sustainability and strategic flexibility, continuity and change, the cathedral and the bazaar, is the big challenge for all organizations of the future. Investing in individual and organizational coaching holds network organizations together, while allowing them to breathe with change and transition.

Any other comments?

None.

Contact details

Claudia Velazco
Tel: +49 89 636 43720
e-mail: claudia.velazco@siemens.com

CASE STUDY 4

What examples do you have of using coaching to support change or transform performance?

I run a workshop for Vodafone UK focusing on work/life balance and transformational leadership. It takes the form of coaching a group of 15, accompanied by individual coaching sessions where necessary. The purpose is to enable each delegate to achieve an effective work/life balance that provides maximum benefit to both the company and the individual. For the benefits to be maintained it is imperative to ensure the learning is something each delegate takes on board as a true behavioural change, rather than just being a methodology that has to be consciously applied. Three months after the end of the programme the delegates have to write a report explaining how by improving their own work/life balance and personal satisfaction there has also been a considerable financial benefit to the company.

This case study looks at the experience of Debbie, who is a regional retail manager and a single mother of three. She was spending a lot of extra hours on work in order to feel she was on top of it, and consequently fewer hours at home with her children. This case study contains perspectives of the process from both Debbie and myself.

What were the biggest challenges?

Debbie

- Putting into practice the theories and models used to manage work/life balance.
- Time management – *actually* creating the time to make it work.
- Understanding the impact of how it could change my lifestyle.
- My own personal fear that by using the new practices my life could have been a lot better balanced before – so there was a lot of soul searching and acceptance that life is all about learning and it never stops,

and it's not that I was doing it wrong before but that a new way is just more effective.

- I had used work as a crutch for a long time and would now be having to deal with 'real life'.
- Accepting constructive feedback on my own style, on me.
- Taking on board others' comments, instant perceptions of me and what impact I could make/had made.
- Learning to listen, stop, reflect and act – and actually making the time to do it.
- Learning to like myself – my personal life affecting my self-esteem and morale, and actually hearing that I was OK and that by liking myself and not personally berating how I managed work, family, friends I could actually improve all my relationships and be a better mother, daughter, partner, friend, manager, colleague.
- My dedication, focus, time had been around work and I had ignored, even though I was aware of it, the importance and impact my closed approach to personal matters was having – if I stopped then I would have to deal with it and that is where the initial fear comes from – stopping, taking stock and realizing that the priorities had been in the wrong areas of my life.
- I can do the work day job – what if I couldn't do the personal balance? Being competent, recognized, accepted in my work life made me question could I really do the life/personal job – juggling it was the norm, but actually dealing with it?
- Could I do it?

The coach

- Debbie's cynicism of the benefits of life coaching.
- Her fear of changing a well-honed strategy of control that covered up stress and dissatisfaction, to replace it with one that would force her to look at other options that she hadn't tried and tested.
- Her negative opinion of herself and her abilities, and her low self-esteem.

How did you overcome these?

Debbie

My coach overcame these by:

- Having faith in my abilities and communicating them back to me.
- Understanding my fears – even when I hadn't articulated them and even when I sometimes wasn't certain what they were!
- Making it all clear, simple, practicable and user friendly.
- Questioning – me, my lifestyle, my goals and aspirations.
- Giving me the time to make my own decisions.
- Using various models and theories and allowing me to choose the ones that fitted. One example was exploring a person's behaviour versus their intention. This blew me away. As a simple thought process it allows a better, calmer approach and understanding of an individual/group interaction and has most definitely helped me develop and understand people's behaviours.
- Allowing me the time for trial and error.

The coach

I overcame her cynicism by building up her trust with me – allowing her the time to see that what I had to say made sense, and allowing her to go away and think about it. By having her create a realistic and personal vision of what things would be like for herself, the company and her loved ones if she carried on as she was, I helped to overcome her fear of leaving some of her old strategies behind to take on new, more effective ones. I run an exercise that has people realize that they can control what they do with their time, and that time is precious. It is a big motivator to ensure people are filling their time with activities that are meaningful for them. Debbie says about this:

> the scariest moment was the review of our life – the walk and where are you now. Because it was made into a physical exercise it brought home the reality of what we can accomplish with the time we have left and there being very little of it, so time is a precious commodity and one that we effectively waste each day.

Having Debbie take personal responsibility for her choices and their impact was the key to turning everything around.

What have been the benefits?

Debbie

My whole demeanour has changed:

- I'm calmer, more approachable, most certainly a better time manager, focused, don't procrastinate, more proactive, better listener, more aware of others around me and what impact I can have by my personal language patterns and also my behaviour.
- I care, genuinely care, about others, what they can offer and what I can give back.
- I don't make assumptions until I have explored, listened and questioned.
- I bite my tongue – a lot! This is good for others around me.
- Actually having a work/life balance and enjoying it.
- Professionally working smarter but not harder – effective in the time I am paid to work (still not got down to exactly 40 hours per week but managing the day job in under 50!).
- Displaying better behaviours, which are now commented on by my colleagues, staff and line managers.
- I have more financial control! This has been achieved by better planning, being more organized – no guilty purchases for working late and having to buy the affections of others!

- I don't squeeze time (ie by not doing five non-effective store visits per day but one *very* productive and effective store visit) – I work with the time I have got – priority management.
- Personally – have met my children halfway – we all own our family relationship and they now do creative planning, mind mapping, are calmer and more supportive – I feel less guilty, for when I work I can concentrate on the task and know that when I am home I am there in body and mind! Not as previously just the body!
- I have a new man in my life – one who had been there for nine years and I had never noticed!

The coach

As well as the observable benefits to Debbie, any coaching (however quick and informal) I do with her now is so much easier for me and for her. The process becomes faster and smoother.

What advice would you give to others?

The coach

For people to change the way they are doing things there has to be a genuine desire for something else. If there isn't, then the motivation for working at it won't be high, and the chance of maintaining the results will be low. Ensure clients are in a state where they are truly hungry for what you are helping them towards. Individuals may express a need to change for all sorts of reasons that aren't about true desire, eg peer pressure, doing what the boss says, boredom, and in those cases the coaching process usually won't work very well. That desire will come from something deep inside people, and there will be an emotional response to the thought of it. If you are not sure your clients have a real desire, or have the right attitude, to personal change then first find the emotional 'hook' that will facilitate it before starting on the process of getting them there.

Any other comments?

Debbie

Certain models had the greatest impact and are tools that I genuinely use daily.

The coach

There is a range of models and techniques that I use frequently to help move clients forward as quickly and effectively as possible, but those alone do not create personal change. It is the flexibility of their use and application, the selection of the right technique for each unique situation, and the sensitivity towards the client as an individual that create success. It is the skilful combination of those things that make for a great coaching outcome.

Contact details

Deborah Moran
Director, Epona Associates Ltd
e-mail: deb@eponaassociates.co.uk
Web site: www.eponaassociates.co.uk

CASE STUDY 5

What examples do you have of using coaching to support change or transform performance?

As part of its broad objective of supporting organizational learning, the United Nations Development Programme (UNDP) launched the Learning Manager Network (a global network of learning coaches) concept in October 1999 as a way to better support the global development of staff competencies, with individual self-directed learning as the anchor. Three years on, over 95 per cent of all 140-plus country offices have learning managers/learning coaches. As participants in specifically designed action-learning-based learning manager workshops, the majority of learning managers have undergone coaching training to equip them with the basic competencies required for their challenging role as change agents for learning. In that context, newly appointed learning managers, most of whom were totally new to the concept of coaching, were coached one to one, experienced group coaching and had an opportunity to practise coaching themselves in order to learn how to coach their clients back in their duty stations as opposed to becoming merely experts for learning. At all times, the learning manager function is supplemented by support from headquarters as well as through exchanges and peer support within the Learning Manager Network (LMN) itself. The LMN has become a community of practice that has evolved into one of the most vibrant and largest of UNDP's networks. The LMN is a determined group of learning coaches who have volunteered (and been nominated/supported by their managers) to support and advocate for staff learning in addition to their other functions.

What were the biggest challenges?

1. Creating a largely decentralized and virtually operating network where ongoing trust was the underlying source for successful reciprocal learning and mutual collaboration.

2. Resisting the temptation of planning every detail and enforcing the implementation of every planned detail on the list in the roll-out of this project as opposed to going with the flow. For example, ensuring the natural growth of the network based largely on interest of the (self-nominating) learning managers as opposed to enforcing top-down nominations of candidates.
3. Respecting the diversity of the group and allowing for different learning manager approaches in different cultures, by different people with different skills and in a different work context.
4. Ensuring continuous collaboration amongst all the members of the network after their return to their duty stations.

How did you overcome these?

1. By embedding the learning managers into a learning process where they begin to experience the power of the network from day one of their nomination, and bringing them together for the action-learning-based face-to-face workshop (a completely customized workshop designed to address the needs of each and every participant) and their coaching training very early in the process.
2. By establishing broad goals, like the expected coverage, with learning managers, and at the same time responding quickly to emerging detail issues even if they were not on the initial plan, such as support to a regional meeting or quick and unbureaucratic support to a new learning manager who has replaced somebody who had just been trained. Also being willing to let go and respecting silent periods or virtual disappearances.
3. By emphasizing that each learning manager has the right and duty to determine, based on his or her personal situation, what can be done on the ground and what can't. The corporate learning function provides the framework and support mechanisms. Rather than mandating the implementation of certain activities across the board, which often leads to frustration, this sort of situational performance management approach leads to an empowerment of the incumbent and to a motivation that

results in a much more dedicated effort (self-directed), ultimately with much higher impact.

4. By providing continuous support to the network via electronic media, from telephone to collaboration technology. Making staff time available to deal with emerging issues and at all times modelling the behaviours expected from them. Ensuring quick turnaround when support is requested. Undertaking occasional visits to country offices and giving pep-talks about learning to support the learning manager role. Enhancing the visibility of the LMN in the internal and external context. Fostering sub-regional collaboration amongst learning managers: the management of the project needs to stay in touch with the group as a whole. Making uninvited contributions to the network, sending out documents, sharing information, commenting on something positive that happened elsewhere in the LMN.

What have been the benefits?

The support the members of the network have been giving each other can hardly be expressed other than in the stories from the trenches but it has been very, very real. The activities within the network vary from a quick 'Happy Birthday' note, to a recommendation for a consultant, to badly needed moral support in a difficult situation. From an impact point of view, the learning managers by now have become strong allies of the central learning function and, on top of delivering ongoing learning support on a global scale but locally adapted, they are increasingly called upon to get involved with corporate initiatives such as the roll-out of a new performance assessment process, the roll-out of the online computer driver's licence (ICDL) and the 360 feedback programme. Thanks to their dedicated work, 59 per cent of UNDP staff confirm having spent at least 5 per cent of their work time in 2003 on learning (up from 53 per cent the year before) and they answered yes to the question as to whether they receive the training needed to do a quality job in the Global Staff Survey 2003. A total of 66 per cent now say 'My supervisor encourages me to take advantage of learning opportunities', as compared with 62 per cent last year and only 50 per cent two years ago.

What advice would you give to others?

Managing such a network is like coaching an extremely diverse group of people at three different levels at the same time, namely individual support, group support and a focus on creating organizational impact. Trust the process and provide ongoing support (yourself and your team) at all of these levels simultaneously with a view to empowering the whole group rather than solving their problems. In the end, this will be a perfect approach to solving your main challenge: ensuring the enhancement of organizational learning.

Any other comments?

All learning managers are fully aware that change happens at different levels – individual, group and organizational. Therefore they are each trained to find their personal entry points for best results at any of these levels. Since the situation in each country office is different, it is important to accept that what represents the challenge in one office might already be an achievement in another office and vice versa. This is exactly where the power of the network becomes most obvious. Sharing and mutual support in their everyday functions, at any of the three levels, are at the heart of the LMN. Whether the challenge is of a personal nature, such as becoming a better listener, whether it is related to the group/office level, such as how to best promote the use of learning resources in a particular office, or whether it is organizational, such as how to advocate for the 5 per cent of staff time for learning, the learning managers can safely rely on the respectful support of their peers.

Contact details

Gunnar Brückner, former Chief Learning Officer, United Nations Development Programme, and presently CEO of coachingplatform Inc
Berlin Office: +49 30 2101 4077
Global cell phone: +49 171 744 2612
e-mail: gunnar.bruckner@coachingplatform.com
Web site: http://coachingplatform.com

United Nations Development Programme (UNDP)
Office of Human Resources/Learning Resources Center (LRC)
c/o Maria Drago
304 East 45th Street
New York, NY 10017
e-mail: maria.drago@undp.org

9

Coaching for change – a summary of the key stages

At the start of this book it was stated that coaching for change is about creating a process of learning that supports each individual's capacity to grow and that personal growth should equate with organizational growth. The corporate effect of individual transformation of performance should be enhanced organization performance, but this will only occur if the individual identifies with the overall goals of the organization.

If you find yourself with an opportunity to become a business partner in a transformation process there are some key steps that you can undertake to make a successful contribution:

1. Embrace the opportunity.
2. Recognize that the going will get tough.
3. Develop a strong network to support you both in and out of work.
4. Work in partnership with the business and any external partners involved in the process.
5. Use the experience as a learning opportunity; keep a log of the progress; identify the issues and solutions.
6. If you are involved in designing the people development, map it as a journey; clearly identify the start point, the end point and the stages in between.

7. Use tools and techniques to identify the overall objectives, the current strengths and development opportunities.
8. Where appropriate, network with other organizations experiencing the same issues to identify best practice.
9. Internally, encourage the learning and sharing as different parts of the business go through the process.
10. Use it as a real opportunity to transform the learning and development products and services.
11. Be creative; think laterally; do not think 'What have we done before?' but instead 'What could we do differently?'
12. Involve the CEO, the board, line managers in the opportunity to create a coaching culture.
13. Identify the stars, the sponsors, the people who will make it happen.
14. As different parts of the process are completed, review the learning, learn from mistakes and celebrate the successes.

Introducing coaching is an important step for any organization. However it is not simply the introduction that is important. What is much more critical is sustaining it, nourishing it and taking the commitment seriously.

Coaching in itself is just a word, but behind that word lies the very real opportunity for leaders to share wisdom and knowledge and create a culture that values the contribution of each and every employee.

Managers who coach have the opportunity to inspire, excite and develop teams of motivated employees.

Individuals who are coached and who coach their colleagues have the opportunity to embark on a voyage of self-discovery where they are able to fulfil their real potential.

The organizations of the future need to recognize the importance of retaining talent, of helping people to create a work/life balance and of tailoring learning to the needs of the individual.

CHAPTER SUMMARIES

Here is a summary of the key points raised in each chapter.

Chapter 1: Creating a process of change

So how do you support transforming performance? The answer to this can be highly complex, or surprisingly simple, depending on your approach. I have tried to adopt a simple but thorough model of Five Principles to transform performance:

1. Accurately assess the readiness to change.
2. Clearly state the overall strategic direction.
3. Identify the key stages on the journey.
4. Gain commitment to the common goal.
5. Establish a process to learn and grow.

Chapter 2: Creating a coaching landscape

There are key areas to focus on:

1. Identify organizational readiness for coaching.
2. Identify potential coaches.
3. The role of the coach.
4. Develop the right attitudes and behaviours.
5. Equipping the coaches with the right skills and knowledge.
6. Encourage coaching to support the change process.
7. Learn from the experience; share the wisdom.

Chapter 3: Motivation to change

1. What is stopping me?
2. What would I do differently?
3. What could I do today to help me take the first step towards achieving my vision?
4. What help will I need?
5. Who do I know that I trust to talk to about what I want to achieve?
6. What will happen to me if I don't get started?
7. If I decide to wait what are my reasons?
8. If I am going to wait when will it be the right time?
9. What have been the best successes in my life?
10. What can I learn from these successes to help me achieve my current vision and goals?

Chapter 4: Organizational change

How to become great – key characteristics:

1. Know where you are going; understand the big picture; develop an over-arching plan.
2. Temper this with compassion – recognize your position in the community and address your corporate social responsibility.
3. Be entrepreneurial – seize opportunities to do business and make money.
4. Have a desire and drive to succeed – be energized, committed.
5. Recognize and respect your employees' strengths, talents and emotional intelligence; look to identify the great leaders.

6. Be positive, optimistic; overcome setbacks.
7. Be imaginative, inventive, curious; what shall we do next?
8. Be able to learn from the past, reinvent, regenerate, draw from what is good and discard what doesn't work.
9. Benchmark, measure and celebrate success.
10. Network and partner with others.

Chapter 5: The role of the coach

Coaches do the following:

- They build a positive environment.
- They ask questions to analyse needs.
- They use open questions to probe.
- They focus on the needs of the individual.
- They offer suggestions to build on the views expressed by learners.
- They listen actively.
- They seek ideas and build on them.
- They give feedback.
- They agree action plans for development.
- They monitor performance.
- They give ongoing support.
- They focus on improving performance in the current job.
- They assist in raising performance to the required standards.
- They emphasize the present.

Chapter 6: Coaching conversations

- *Where am I now?*
  - What skills, competencies have I achieved?
  - What job role?
  - What about development on the job, off job?
  - Who offers me support currently?
- *What would I like to do differently in the future?*
  - What style and pattern of working?
  - What new responsibilities?
  - What job change?
  - Do I want to transfer to another part of the business?
  - What about location?
  - What skills, competencies, training or new learning do I need?
- *What are my work-related goals?*
  - In three months' time I would like to have...
  - In six months' time I would like to have...
  - In 12 months' time I would like to have...
  - How would I break these goals down into SMART objectives?
  - How could I push myself further?
- *What would I like to achieve outside work?*
  - What are my hopes and aspirations?
  - What is realistic to achieve in the short term?
  - How could I break these down into bite-sized achievable goals?
  - Who will offer me support?
  - How will I measure my success?

Chapter 7: Coaching the new learners

1. Identify the core learning need.
2. Establish the level of demand/timescales.
3. Recognize the different learning styles.
4. Look creatively at the potential of using different forms of learning, eg matching the learning need to different delivery methods and identifying the best fit.
5. Work with the current providers, internal and external, to identify the learning objectives and to ensure that the provision meets the current need.
6. Undertake an education process to illustrate the potential of different types of learning.
7. Be prepared to offer follow-up coaching support.
8. Set up a monitoring process to evaluate the effectiveness of the delivery.

WHAT ARE THE IMPLICATIONS FOR ORGANIZATIONS?

Here are some recommendations:

- Be committed to and respect all your human capital.
- Encourage and develop diversity within your workforce.
- Don't just pay lip-service to the concept of talent management. Focus on it and demonstrate your commitment from the very top of your organization.
- Recognize the importance of your employer brand. Demonstrate your values and brand in the way that you conduct your business and develop your people.

- Create an honest, positive and thinking environment.
- Develop your emotional intelligence.
- Be committed to identifying and recognizing talent at all levels in your organization.
- Give individuals freedom to innovate, generate ideas and receive feedback.
- Develop coaching and feedback processes throughout your organization.
- Create an environment that attracts potential employees to want to come and work for you.
- Create internal forums that allow for healthy debate and discussion.
- Encourage flexible and imaginative patterns of employment.
- Ensure that your management structure is developing new talent and creating a coaching and learning culture.
- Encourage all employees to be committed to developing your talent pool.
- Make an ongoing commitment to your community in deeds as well as donations.

THE IMPLICATIONS FOR INDIVIDUALS

Focus on becoming a person with influence. If you are looking to develop others, to build a coaching culture, it is important that you build your own inner resilience, that you are confident, that you develop self-belief and, most importantly, that *you become the person you always aspired to be*.

There are a number of references within this book to becoming a business partner. If you want to become an effective business partner think about the following:

- Build your own inner resilience.
- Have the confidence to manage your own career.
- Develop self-belief.
- Become a person of influence.
- Seek to become a business partner.
- Take responsibility for your own development.
- Be curious.
- Develop the courage and wisdom to push against the corporate boundaries.
- Want to make a difference in your organization and in the wider community.
- Set yourself stretching personal targets and goals.
- Regularly research new areas of development.
- Build an extensive network of colleagues and business acquaintances.

THE IMPLICATIONS FOR MANAGERS

Managers have a major role to play in the development of a coaching culture. They can sponsor individuals; they can free up channels of communication; they can foster an environment of trust and integrity.

- Set yourself stretching personal targets and goals.
- Give open and honest feedback.
- Set clear goals and targets with your team.
- Lead by example.
- Create open lines of communication.

- Sponsor individual development.
- Be prepared to listen.
- Encourage people to take responsibilities and give them freedom to operate.
- Seek to build relationships.
- Create a coaching environment.
- Take responsibility for developing new talent.
- Encourage innovation and creativity.
- Recognize the contribution of people who are different.
- Foster an environment in which individuals are valued and nurtured.

SUMMARY OF KEY POINTS IN THE PROCESS OF TRANSFORMATION

1. Recognize the reality of what you're trying to do.
2. Be brave but not foolish.
3. Carefully research how others have achieved it. Build on their findings but create your own plan.
4. Always keep your overall route map close by, ready to show others and to reinforce your own beliefs.
5. Don't try to do it alone; identify key members of a support team and keep in close communication.
6. Break the journey up into bite-size chunks and set key deliverables.
7. Review each stage and learn the lessons from what has worked and what hasn't.
8. Don't be afraid to amend the plan in the light of the lessons learnt.
9. Don't let apparent difficulties or failure overwhelm you; have contingency plans.

10. People often give up when they are closest to achieving their goals. Take regular breaks, do something different and return with new energy.
11. Listen to feedback but make sure it is balanced.
12. Recognize that not everyone is able to make the journey. Support people as they make the difficult choices.
13. Use your own support network, personal coach and mentor.
14. Do not over-analyse failure; learn from it and move on.
15. Celebrate success and prepare for the next stage of the journey.

To conclude, there follows an extract from *Walking in This World* by Julia Cameron (2002):

> Chekhov advised actors, 'If you want to work on your career work on yourself.' It might equally be advised, if you want to work on yourself, work to make your career of service to something larger than yourself. Dedicate yourself to something, or someone other than yourself. This expansion will make you larger both as a person, and as an artist.

She adds this quotation,

> Whatever you can do or dream you can, begin it. Boldness has genius, power and magic to it.
>
> (Johann Wolfgang von Goethe)

I hope you have found this book useful, and I wish you every success in your own journey of transformation.

References

Bennis, W and Biedermann, P W (1997) *Organizing Genius*, Nicholas Brealey, London

Cameron, Julia (2002) *Walking in This World*, Rider, London

Coelho, Paul (1993) *The Alchemist*, Harper, San Francisco

Goleman, Daniel (1999) *Working with Emotional Intelligence*, Bloomsbury, London

Goleman, Daniel (2002) *The New Leaders*, Little, Brown & Co, London

Handy, Charles (1995) *Beyond Certainty*, Hutchinson, London

Heller, Robert (1998) *In Search of European Excellence*, HarperCollins Business, London

McNally, David (1993) *Even Eagles Need a Push*, Thorsons, London

Patler, Louis (1999) *Don't Compete... Tilt the Field!*, Capstone, Oxford

Peters, Tom (1997) *The Circle of Innovation*, Hodder & Stoughton, London

Semler, Ricardo (1993) *Maverick*, Arrow, London

Semler, Ricardo (2003) *Seven Day Weekend*, Century, London

Slater, Robert (1998) *Jack Welch and the GE Way: Management insights and leadership secrets of the legendary CEO*, McGraw-Hill, New York

Thorne, K (2001) *Personal Coaching: Releasing potential at work*, Kogan Page, London

Thorne, K (2003a) *Blended Learning*, Kogan Page, London

Thorne, K (2003b) *Managing the Mavericks*, Spiro, London

Thorne, K and Machray, A (2000) *World Class Training: Providing training excellence*, Kogan Page, London

Thorne, K and Mackey, D (2003) *Everything You Ever Needed to Know about Training*, 3rd edn, Kogan Page, London

Woodhouse, Mark and Thorne, Kaye (2003) *Talent Management*, Reed Business Information, Surrey

Further reading

Belasco, James A (1990) *Teaching the Elephant to Dance: Empowering change in your organisation*, Hutchinson Business, London

Belbin, Meredith B (1981) *Management Teams*, Heinemann, London

Black, Jack (1994) *Mindstore*, Thorsons, London

Bohm, David and Nichol, Lee (1996) *On Dialogue*, Routledge, London

Buzan, Tony (1995) *Use Your Head*, 4th edn, BBC, London

Buzan, Tony and Buzan, Barry (1993) *The Mind Map Book*, BBC, London

CBI in association with KPMG (2001) *Intellectual Property: A business guide*, CBI, London

Csikzentmihalyi, Mihalyi (1990) *Flow*, Harper & Row, New York

De Bono, E (1999) *Six Thinking Hats*, Little, Brown & Co, Boston, MA

Dyson, J (1998) *Against the Odds: An autobiography*, Trafalgar Square, London

Gardner, H (1993) *Frames of Mind*, Basic Books, New York

Handy, Charles (1994) *The Empty Raincoat*, Hutchinson, London

Helmstetter, Shad (1998) *What to Say When You Talk to Yourself*, Cynus

Jaworski, Joe and Senge, Peter (1998) *Synchronicity* , Berrett-Koeler, San Francisco

Kanter, Rosabeth M (1983) *The Change Masters*, Allen & Unwin, London

Kanter, Rosabeth M (1989) *When Giants Learn to Dance*, Simon & Schuster, London

Kao, John (1996) *Jamming: The art and discipline of business creativity*, Harper Collins, London

Kolb, David A, Rubin, I M and McIntyre, J M (1994) *Organisational Psychology: An experiential approach to organisational behavior*, 4th edn, Prentice Hall, London

LeBoeuf, Michael (1976) *Creative Thinking*, Piatkus, London

O'Connor, Joseph and Seymour, John (1990) *Introducing NLP Neuro Linguistic Programming*, Mandala, London

O'Connor, Joseph and Seymour, John (1994) *Training with NLP: Skills for managers, trainers and communicators*, Thorsons, London

Peters, Tom (1992) *Liberation Management*, Knopf, New York

Peters, Tom, and Austin, Nancy (1985) *A Passion for Excellence*, Collins, London

Ridderstråle, J and Nordstrom, K (2000) *Funky Business*, ft.com, London

Salovey, P, Mayer, J D and Caruso, D R (1997) Emotional intelligence meets traditional standards for an intelligence, unpublished manuscript

Senge, Peter M (1990) *The Fifth Discipline*, Doubleday, New York

Index